Hostile CRAVINGS

Hostile CRAVINGS

WICKED CRAVINGS
BOOK THREE

JL JACKOLA

Paperback ISBN 978-1-960784-56-8
Electronic ISBN 978-1-960784-57-5

Distributed by Tivshe Publishing
Printed in the United States of America

Cover design by Tivshe Publishing

Visit www.jljackola.com

Also by J. L. Jackola

UNBOUND PROPHECY SERIES

Ascension

Descent

Surfacing

Submerged

Riven

Adrift

UNBOUND PROPHECY NOVELS

Unbound Kingdom (the trilogy omnibus)

Orlaina (an Unbound Prophecy prequel)

UNBOUND KINGDOM TRILOGY

Severed Kingdom

Cursed Kingdom

Prophesied Kingdom

WICKED HUES SERIES

The Forgotten Hues of Skye

The Coveted Hues of Skye

The Shattered Shades of Crimson

The Impossible Shades of Crimson

The Endless Shadows of Pete

Author's Note

Welcome back to the world of wicked cravings where morally gray is the norm and cravings are hard to resist.

Hostile Cravings is a mafia romance with dark aspects, so be prepared to expect:

Explicit sexual content
Language
Threats of sexual assault (not by the mmc)
Violence and death

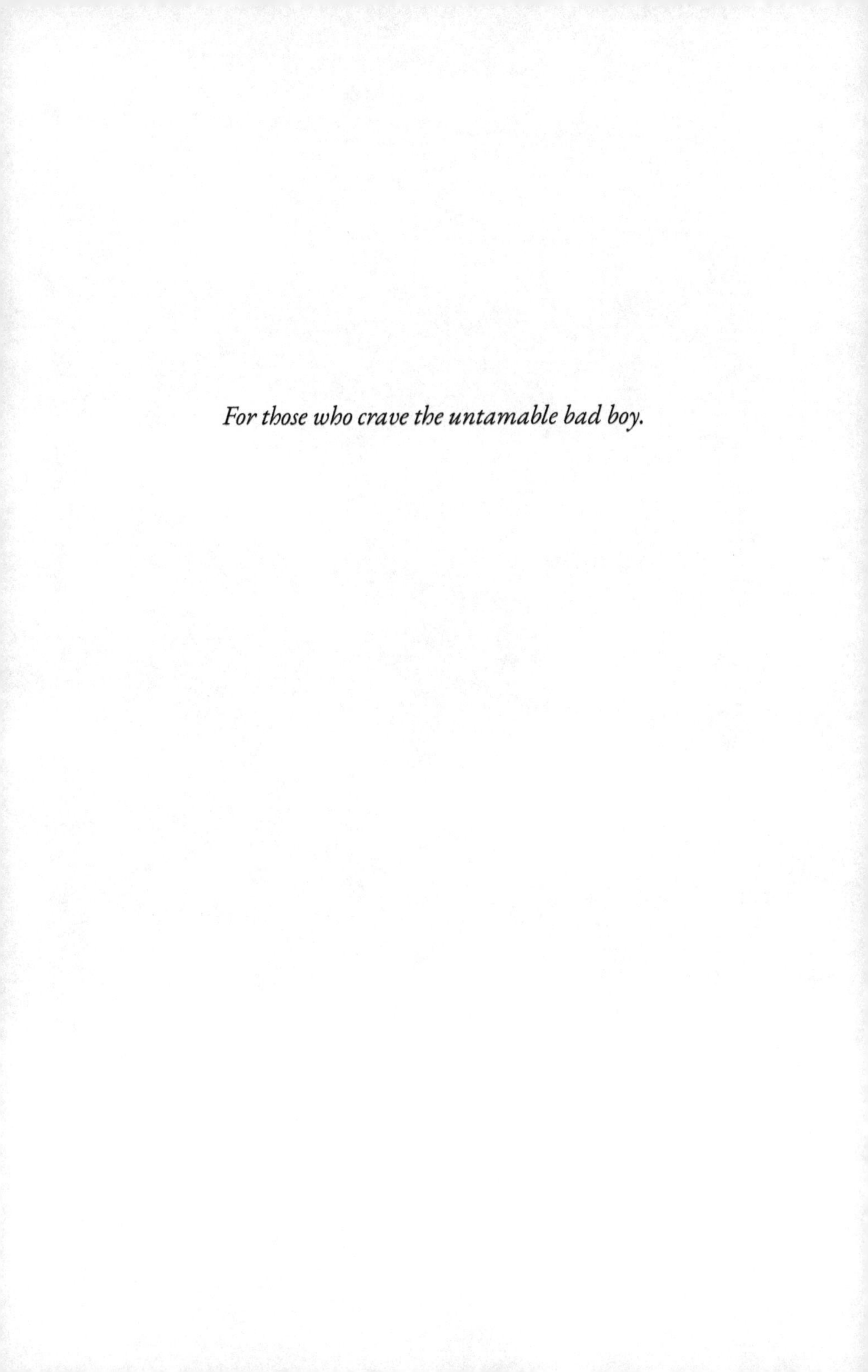

For those who crave the untamable bad boy.

TYSON

This was a nightmare. I pulled the lapels of my jacket, wishing I had some way to escape but knowing there was no way out. Each time my foot hit the tile floor of the Donelli mansion, it echoed like a steady beat of drums that was building to my doom. Fuck Mason for agreeing to this and fuck Donelli and his shithead son for even suggesting it. Rolling my neck, I approached the deck that overlooked the wide expanse of the Donelli estate, the shimmering pool water below inviting me to plunge into it rather than deal with this dreadful situation.

Angie Donelli. Of all the women Mason could have forced on me, it had to be that one. Spoiled, bratty, mouthy, unappreciative...the list was one that never ended. She annoyed the shit out of me and even being in her presence for mere minutes sent my anger rising and my head pounding.

Mason was certainly testing my limits as his best friend. First with Casey, now with this. Casey was a matter that had taken me by surprise, hitting me hard. The betrayal had stung. That he hadn't been honest with me had stung harder. But then, even if he had told me up front, I still would have beaten the shit out of him for touching my sister.

My jaw twitched at the thought of him touching her. The thought of anyone touching my sister stirred my ire, but this was Mason. The man who had been by my side since we were kids. A man I trusted with my life and one I trusted with Casey because I knew he would take a bullet for her, just like he would for me. If it had to be anyone, he was the best choice, and I'd come to terms with that. I still wasn't comfortable with how often his hands were on her, but I supposed I'd get used to it. Maybe.

As I stepped onto the deck, I heard Angie's annoying voice along with a male's. Damn, the sham was only beginning, and she was already at it with another man. She was going to be hard to contain, but if I had to give up my women for this, she'd have to do the same. Mason liked to call me a playboy, but Angie Donelli made me look like a virgin. She was a slut who couldn't keep her legs closed, especially for the rich and powerful in her province. She had a taste for money and prestige and expectations that I was sure none of those pussies she slept with met. The pretty boys were her style, and I was far from that. I was rough around the edges and dangerous. Another reason this fake marriage idea was ridiculous. Not only did the two of us hate each other, we were complete opposites.

Rolling my neck, I scanned the deck, squinting my eyes against the setting sun.

"Come on, Angie. You know you want it. Every time you flick that tongue over your lips, you make me hard."

I recognized that voice. Joey Tirenti, the piece of work son of Joseph Tirenti. The Tirenti's ruled the territory just north of Donelli's. They were trouble, and their allegiance to Mason was wavering. The only reason they hadn't turned on us was the debt they owed Mason for bailing their business out years ago. Still, the situation was tenuous, especially with the recent Bad Omen activity. I suspected they were ready to sell their souls to the Omens, as did Mason, but the proof hadn't surfaced yet.

"I don't lick my lips for you, Joey. So get your hands off me."

Great. Tony, Angie's brother, had said he'd caught Joey touching her when she hadn't invited it and from the irritated tone in her high-pitched voice, it was clear she wanted him to leave her alone. It was time to put my acting skills to the test and pray I didn't burst out laughing.

I turned the corner, spotting them. He had her pinned against the side of the house, his hand on her bare leg, his body so far against hers that she couldn't move.

"She only licks them for me, asshole. Now get your hands off my wife." Every word pissed me off, and the effect made my voice sound gritty.

Angie's brown eyes flicked to mine, going wide before understanding crossed them. I had hoped her brother and father had told her their plan. Tony had taken the reins of the family after his near-death experience with the Omens, agreeing with his father that tying Angie with me would affirm their standing after the Omens had attacked them. It was risky, but Mason and I weren't ones to fuck with, and every family knew that. The only ones who held more power were Greyson Tides and the Bad Omen. No one aligned with the Omens and Tides was now in line with us because of Riley.

Joey stepped back from Angie, smoothing his shirt down before he turned to me. His blue eyes were beady, the smirk on his face one I wanted to punch. I had at least five inches on him and my hours in the gym showed in the tight fit of my suit. He was no match for me, and he knew it. I kept my hands in pocket, worried I'd do something stupid if I removed them too soon.

"Raines," he sneered. "I don't see no ring on her finger."

I pulled the box from my pants pocket and tossed it to Angie, who fumbled to catch it. Shit, she was even uncoordinated. As together as she tried to make herself seem, even that was fake. The box flopped to the floor with a thud, and I raised a brow as she threw me an annoyed look.

Joey glanced between the two of us.

"It was a hasty wedding, and I didn't have time for my jeweler to design a ring," I said as Angie bent down to get the box, her tits spilling over her tank top. If they weren't on her, I would have been all for reaching my hands in and touching them. But they were, and as hot as she was, she wasn't worth messing with. There was nothing about her that tempted me enough to take on that personality that grated on my nerves like fingers on a chalkboard.

"Not going to put it on my finger, honey?" she said, throwing her blonde hair over her shoulder.

"Yeah, 'honey' why don't you put it on her finger like a real man? And where's your ring, Raines?" Joey asked. My fists were ready to meet his jaw, but I kept them clenched. "I'm having a hard time believing Angie would lower her standards for you."

I gritted my teeth, thinking of the scolding Mason would give me if I punched Joey. Shoving him aside, I snatched the box from Angie's hand. I needed to calm down, or I'd blow this, and Mason was expecting me to follow through with it. This wasn't about me and my hatred for the bratty bitch in front of me, it was for the family and securing our place in the hierarchy.

Leaning my hand on the wall above Angie, I brushed my mouth over her ear, noticing how her body went rigid. I may have detested her, but she hated me just as much.

"Did you miss me, little viper?" I murmured. "Play the part, Angie." I said the last words low enough to avoid Joey hearing them.

She relaxed, bringing her hand up my chest, her touch turning my stomach. "More than I realized," she purred, her fingers moving up to my hair and threading through it before she turned her face so our lips met.

That had been unexpected, and it threw me off guard. The kiss was stiff and uncomfortable, but still she parted her lips. I knew Joey was watching, so with the hand that still held the ring box, I grabbed her waist and pulled her against me. My tongue met hers, strangely intrigued by how inviting she was.

"Damn you, Raines. I can guarantee your whore was locking those lips around another man's cock when she was clubbing last night, so don't think she won't be locking them on mine."

I released her, quick to stop the awkward kiss and not liking how hard I'd grown from it. Reminding myself that this was Angie and not someone I wanted, I shook the feeling off.

"Hold this," I said to her, handing her the box before turning to Joey.

As truthful as I knew his words were because Angie was like me, hard to contain when it came to sex, I didn't like what he'd said. Even if I hated her, I'd been dealing with her family long enough to be protective of her. I could insult her, but not this jackass.

He lifted his chin, his bravado high. "You got a problem with that, Raines?"

Grabbing him by the collar, I threw him against the wall. He tried to recover, but I was on him too fast.

"Apologize to her quickly before my fist meets your face and I have to explain to your father how disrespectful you were to my wife."

Every time I said the word wife, it was like a punch in my gut.

"I don't need to apologize for anything, not when I'm speaking the truth. She fucks anything."

"I won't fuck you, asshole," she snapped.

I laughed. "See, she does have some standards."

"She's a whore—"

My punch hit him quick, and he slid to floor, holding his nose which had cracked under the pressure of my fist.

"Call her a whore again and I'll wreck the rest of your face up so bad your old man won't recognize you."

I snatched Angie's hand and dragged her from the deck. My fury was raging through me. I'd lost my temper with Joey and it would cause even more friction than this sham marriage would. Angie whined behind me, and I jerked her closer, ignoring her until we reached her room where I threw the door open and pushed her in.

"You can't treat me like this, Tyson," she complained, rubbing her wrist.

"I'll treat you any way I want. Have you really been screwing your random hook-ups at the clubs knowing we were doing this?"

She huffed, crossing her tan arms. "Doing this? You mean tying me down to your ugly ass for some indefinite time? Cutting me off for who knows how long? And don't think your dick is getting anywhere near me."

I grabbed her by the neck and pushed her against the dresser, hearing her breath hitch.

"Trust me, my dick doesn't want to be anywhere near you. You couldn't handle me even if you tempted me. I'm not one of your pretty boys. I'm cut different and when I fuck, it's hard and dirty." I squeezed her neck, noting how her lips parted. There was something in her eyes, a mix of vile hatred and lust, and I wasn't sure what to make of it. "We're both cut off from what we like. Trust me, I'm not keen on giving up my women just to keep that asshole from touching you. But I will, just like you will. And if I find another man's hands on you while we do this, I'll cut them off and make you sleep next to them until this is over."

I released her and walked away, running my hands through my hair before I reached down and picked up the ring box she'd dropped when I grabbed her.

"I hate you, Tyson," she snarled.

"Feeling's mutual, Anj." Pulling the rings out, I walked back to her and snatched her hand. "But your father and brother think you need my protection. And now you're stuck with me." I shoved the band and the engagement ring Casey had picked out for me onto Angie's finger. "Till death do us part."

"You don't have to be so rough," she complained once they were on.

"I like it rough, baby, so be thankful this is fake, or you'd be too sore in the morning to walk."

I turned from her, intent on leaving the room.

"I don't mind it rough," she mumbled.

Shaking my head, I glanced over at her. She looked a little wounded, like I'd hurt her feelings, but she quickly covered it, the bitch I knew returning.

"I doubt you know what rough is, little viper. You're still too young and those men you let touch you aren't like me. Pack your things. You're coming home with me, regardless of what either of us wants."

I left her there, thinking about how true my words were. She was young, younger even than Casey. At twenty-five, she was eleven years my junior. Her immaturity showed in everything she did, from her clubbing to her conceited need to have the attention on her all the time. Running my hand through my hair, I wondered how I was going to make this work without killing her. There was a high probability I would, and that was a risk, almost as much of a risk as trying to pull off the idea that I was in love with a woman I despised.

Chapter Two

ANGIE

Damn my brother for agreeing with my father. This idea of theirs was the worst. Tyson Raines. Even his name turned my stomach. I wiped my mouth with the back of my hand and stomped over to my closet, muttering curses at the bastard. The thought of having to live with him, to pretend we were something other than two people who hated each other, was enough to make me vomit.

I grabbed a suitcase, my closet light illuminating the large diamond ring that sat above the wedding band he'd shoved on my finger. Dropping the suitcase on my bed, I studied the two rings. They were stunning, exactly what I would have picked out, and I could only assume Casey had helped him choose them. Shaking my head, I wiped my hands over my shorts, trying not to think about them, but the unfamiliar weight on my finger was too hard to ignore.

With a huff, I sat on my bed, staring across the room into my walk-in closet and having no idea what to pack. I didn't know how long this was going to last. I had never been out of our province with its constant warmth, sunny days, the beaches and my pool occupying the time I didn't spend at my father's nightclubs.

This was a disaster, and I didn't want to go. I didn't want to be the pretend wife of Tyson Raines. The brute was an asshole. He was rough with his hard eyes, his towering stance, the tattoos that lined his arms, and those muscles that bulged under his shirts. Not that I minded tattoos and muscles, but not his. He hated me and with his hate, my own had festered until neither of us could stand being in the same room with each other.

Now we were stuck together until this thing with the Tirenti's died down. Joey had a lot of nerve touching me. Tony had warned him, but Joey sensed my father's weakness and Tony had yet to assume the authority my father once held. I may not have cared to get involved in the family business, but I knew enough to know if Mason and Tyson weren't offering protection, my father would have fallen long before the Bad Omen incident. With Tony stepping in and having his rebirth, as he called it, there was a chance we could return to the standing we'd once had among the families.

That was about all I knew of the business, and I didn't care to know any more. As long as we had money and I could go through life carefree and having fun, the rest could fall to my brother. It didn't bother me that they all thought I was dumb and naïve. I preferred it that way, to be seen like Tyson saw me—spoiled and bratty.

I looked back down at the ring, wondering why that kiss had burned its way through me once I'd relaxed. Or why the grip around my neck when he'd told me how hard he liked it had soaked me. He was a player, like I was, so I knew he had to be good in bed, but I had no desire to test that theory. Standing, I rubbed my neck, rubbing away his touch and grimacing at the thought of it. I rummaged through my closet, throwing my favorite outfits into the suitcase and filling two more before I was through. I didn't care what Tyson thought of the clothes I brought. He had said I couldn't play, but I doubted he could stop me. There was no way I was going without sex while I was there, and I was damned sure he wouldn't be faithful to this sham marriage.

Tossing a few stilettos and sandals into a bag, I considered the weather in their province might not be as pleasant as ours, but these were the clothes I had. They were all I knew, just like this life. Closing the suitcases, I glanced around my room one last time. Tyson's home was bound to be dull and dreary. Unlike mine where the sun shined constantly and slipped through the sheer pink curtains of my room so that it left stripes over my fuzzy pink comforter. I vaguely wondered if Tyson had anything but depressing colors. Not likely. There was nothing remotely light and carefree about that man.

Leaving my bags in my room, I made my way down the hall, holding my head high and praying I could deal with Tyson Raines without losing my sanity or my life.

RAISED voices drifted through the door of my father's office. He had a rule that I wasn't to interrupt his meetings, but since this one had to do with me, I walked right in. The voices stopped, all eyes turning to me. All but Tyson, whose already clenched fists bunched even tighter, his head sweeping slowly toward me. The hatred in those hazel eyes burned straight through me, but he kept his head tilted away so the others couldn't see.

I lifted my head taller and swished my hips, making my way into the room as if I hadn't a care in the world.

"Pumpkin, what have I told you about interrupting my meetings?"

"But daddy, I know this one's about me," I purred, walking past Tyson and over to my father.

Giving him a kiss on the head, I flipped my hair and turned back to the room. My brother rolled his eyes. Joey looked at me as if I were prey, and his father's lips thinned, but I could see the desire behind them. It made me wonder if Joey had gotten his way, if his father would have taken a piece of me as well. He wasn't as old as my father, but it was still gross. I liked older men, but he fell beyond my taste.

"I think her timing is perfect," he said, his eyes narrowing. "Why don't you tell us how you're suddenly married to Raines when none of us knew anything of the sort?"

I noticed Tyson cross his arms, his muscles bulging below his jacket. The room held so much tension it was almost hard to breathe. Tyson had three men with him who looked ready to pounce on Tirenti's four men, and my father's men had their hands close to their weapons. Tirenti wasn't buying the story, and it was no wonder. It was ridiculous to think I would change my ways in a matter of weeks and marry a man I hated. Just as ridiculous that Tyson would do the same.

It was time to show my new husband why I commanded such a presence everywhere I went and why I had no trouble wrapping men around my fingers. Every man but him. He turned his eyes back to me, the color in them a mix of dark sage and amber.

"Yeah, little viper. Why don't you tell them why you can't keep your hands off me now."

The way he'd suddenly turned his nasty nickname for me into something sexy bothered me, as did the way it burrowed its way into my body like a claim of ownership. He'd been calling me a viper for years. Usually it hissed through his teeth in a sneer, an insult laced with the deepest hatred. It had never bothered me, and I threw my own insults right back at him. But he'd never added 'little' to it, giving it a completely different meaning when it left his lips.

Ignoring the unsettling effect it had on me, I sashayed my way over to him, draping my fingers over his back as I walked around him. His back was taut with tension, his muscles growing tighter at my touch. Taking his hand, I leaned against him, noting the ring that now sat on his finger and ignoring how he seemed to tower over me. I was tall, but standing next to Tyson made me seem petite.

"I admit, I've always hated Ty," I started, using the nickname his sister used. He squeezed my hand, my knuckles aching from the pressure. "He was like a layer of scum I couldn't remove from the bottom of my shoes. Not like the men in our province who have class and manners. They know how to treat a woman right."

I could sense his eyes on me, but I continued talking. "But then he saved me." I snuggled further against his arm, noticing him tense more. "And I saw him for who he really was."

Every word that fell from my mouth was like coughing up lava, burning me with the acidic lies, and I hoped no one noticed. He hadn't saved me. His sister had, as much as I hated to admit it. I despised violence, which was ironic given the world I lived in. I distanced myself from the violence that kept my family in power, turning a blind eye to it. So when Casey had shot that first man, sending his blood splattering me, I'd wanted to run. But she'd dragged me with her, and I'd watched her shoot every one of those men, their lifeless eyes staring back at me. Seeing death so close had changed something in me I still wrestled with and when I'd killed the two shitheads who'd been ready to kill Casey, I'd struggled with the adrenaline high it had given me. The way I'd enjoyed stealing the life from them had been almost as thrilling as sex.

"And who is that?" Joey asked, sitting forward in his seat. "Because I still don't believe it." He was holding a bag of ice to his nose, bruising forming under his eyes.

He gave me the chills. There was something perverse about Joey Tirenti that made me weary of him. The way his eyes were staring right through me sent a shiver down my spine, and I inadvertently leaned closer to Tyson. I sensed Tyson look down at me before he let go of my hand and pulled me into his side in an unexpected move.

"Stop staring at my girl, Joey, or I'll mess the rest of your face up."

Joey went to rise, but his father stopped him with an abrupt hand before rising from his seat. "Touch my son again, Raines, and I walk out of this room. Now answer the damn question, Angie."

Tyson's body was so rigid, his hold on me so suffocating that I could barely talk. I pushed against him, and he loosened his hold. My next move needed to be perfect, or this sham would fall apart, a war would break out, and I could end up with Joey's hands on me. The thought made me sicker than being this close to Tyson. Because as much as I despised Tyson, I feared Joey Tirenti.

Looking up at Tyson, I turned his face to mine, letting my fingers brush along his firm jaw. The amber in his eyes highlighted the green flecks, and I realized I'd never noticed how beautiful his eyes were. My heart pounded in fear at both that thought and the magnitude of what rested on my next words.

"He's my everything now." My stomach rebelled, and I tried not to get sick. "As I sat in that car when he took me home, I realized my hatred for him had only been a cover for my true emotions. That I loved him, and I never wanted to be away from the safety of his arms again. I confessed my love for him right then."

There was a twinkle of humor behind his eyes before he pulled me closer and said, "She straddled me, and I fucked her so hard she knew no other man would satisfy her again."

I wanted to punch him, but I knew he was playing the part, although he was adding his own sting to it because he was as uncomfortable with this as I was. My father cleared his throat, but stayed silent, something I knew was killing him with the way Tyson had just talked about me. But he had no choice but to let Tyson direct the action.

"Isn't that right, little viper?"

"Mmm, that's right." It was hard to answer because his hand

had moved up my back, his fingers twisting in my hair. Goosebumps lined my skin. I'd been with aggressive men who had firm touches and took me hard, but I suspected they were nothing compared to the intensity that Tyson brought. The thought made me uncomfortably warm, the pull of my hair making me more wet than I wanted to admit.

He shoved my lips to his, our mouths smashing with a force that had me gasping. I couldn't help but kiss him back, not liking how my body responded.

"I think that's enough of that. My sister knows I don't like seeing men touch her, Raines," Tony said, and I could hear the disgust in his voice.

Tyson released me and I teetered slightly, my legs too weak for my liking. But he pulled me against him, keeping me upright. I couldn't think. The way that kiss had worked its way through my body had me discombobulated.

"Any other questions, gentleman?"

Tirenti crossed his arms, looking between the two of us.

"Why am I just hearing about this, Donelli? I set this meeting up between us, and Raines is suddenly here to claim your daughter is his?" He turned on my father, storming over to him. Tony reached for his gun, our men doing the same, but my father rose from his seat, standing tall and facing Tirenti. I had a surge of pride. Almost losing Tony and me had left him wounded, and he hadn't been the same since the events with the Bad Omen weeks earlier. He was aging, one of the original bosses who remained in the provinces. He'd married our mother late after his first wife had been murdered in a territory war, so even though I was only twenty-five, my father was in his seventies. I'd never thought much of it. He'd always been a powerful figure in my life until recently.

Seeing him stand up to Tirenti, proud and terrifying, warmed my heart.

"You dare come into my house and threaten me?" His words

were like gavels dropping, each one stressed with a growl. "I will not have you question me or my family."

"My son wants your daughter, Donelli, and I thought I made that clear."

"That's too bad, Tirenti," Tyson said. "Because she's mine and your son will need to go through me to touch her, and I can promise you that won't happen."

Tirenti snapped his head to Tyson.

"Go home and take Joey with you. He's not laying a finger on my wife."

His muscles flexed on the word wife, and I could sense it was as hard to say as the words I'd said.

Tirenti snapped his jacket and motioned for his men and Joey to leave.

"And Tirenti," Tyson said, stopping him in his tracks. "Keep your son on a tighter leash. I hear he's leaving bruises on the women he plays with and there's talk of bodies in the river with worse marks. Mason doesn't stand for that kind of shit and neither do I."

Tirenti glared at him. He shoved Joey out of the room, then followed, their men right behind them.

The door closed, and we all stood frozen, staring at it and waiting for them to leave the house. I realized I had Tyson's jacket bunched in my hand, clinging to him, my body having slowly moved closer to him with his revelations about Joey. No wonder the man had given me the creeps. And now it made sense why my father had asked for Tyson's help.

Tyson's arm dropped from me, and I quickly pushed away from him, wiping my mouth on the back of my hand and trying to brush the sensation of his body against mine away. He was staring at me as he straightened his jacket.

"You kiss me like that again, and I'll show you what I did to that guy at the hangar when Casey and I were saving your ass," I said.

His jaw tightened and a distinct sneer formed on his lips. "Trust me, I don't plan to. It's like kissing an inexperienced virgin."

I shot him an annoyed look. "You go around having sex with virgins a lot?"

This time, the vein on his forehead popped. "I prefer my women experienced, baby. The men around here may not care, but I do."

"You two are going to be a blast," Tony joked. "You sure you don't want to do this marriage thing here so I can see who kills who first?"

"Nobody's killing anyone," my father groused, rubbing his temples. "You two need to make this work. You promised me, Raines—"

"I didn't promise you anything, Donelli. Mason did, and that's the only reason I'm here putting up with this shit. Tirenti's not gonna back down, which is why I'm taking Angie to Treemont with me. The further we are from his scrutiny, the better. But that guarantees nothing. Watch your back."

"And you watch my daughter," my father said.

"I don't have a choice. Angie, go get your suitcase. We need to leave."

I put my hands on my hips. "Suitcases, and you can go get them. Isn't that why you have all those big muscles? You wouldn't want me breaking a nail before our honeymoon even begins."

"Honeymoon? You're delusional," he said, storming past me and grumbling as he walked from the room.

His men followed him out, leaving me alone with my father and Tony. My father motioned for his men to close the door. I waited for it to shut, biting my tongue because I knew my father wanted privacy.

"You keep that shit up, Angela, and he won't put up with you long enough to make this work," he scolded me.

"Me? Daddy, he's horrible. A low-class brute who—"

My father moved in front of me, anger etched on his features. "Now you listen to me, Angela Rosellina Donelli. I came from an even lower class than Raines came from, working my way up the ranks to stake my place as head of this family. We had nothing, and I worked my ass off to ensure you have everything. You insult his roots, you insult mine. Watch your insults and play the part. I don't care how much you hate him. You're safer with him than you are here."

I dropped my eyes, hating that he was angry at me. My father doted on me, never raising his tone with me, and it stung. "Sorry, Daddy."

He took my cheeks in his hands and raised my face to his. "You are my pride and joy, Angela. You and your brother, and I will do whatever it takes to keep you safe. Until Tony and I can ensure the family is no longer vulnerable, until I can put that creep Joey in his place and I'm assured he can't touch you, you stay close to Raines. He may not like you, but he will protect you."

I nodded, forcing back the tears, knowing my father was sending me away for my safety, no matter how it hurt me to leave him, Tony, and my life.

"Now be a good girl and go wait in the car for your husband."

I tried not to cringe, kissing and hugging him goodbye before doing the same to Tony, who gave me a massive hug.

"Be good, Anj, and don't do anything stupid," Tony said.

"Me?" I said, trying to cover the tears that were still pushing against the back of my eyes.

"Yeah, you."

"Never. I wouldn't think of it." I turned, leaving them behind me and saying, "I wonder if they have any good clubs in Treemont," as two of my father's men followed me out of the room.

"Angie!" Tony yelled, and I shook my head, smiling at how protective my older brother was of me.

Head held high, I made my way to the waiting car, Tyson's henchman opening the door for me. Two of my father's men loaded into the car behind mine, his precaution in case this turned ugly, and Tyson and I irritated each other enough to spark violence. It seemed silly since he was handing me over to Tyson as if I was nothing more than a prized horse he was selling.

As I waited for Tyson to join me, I stared out the window, thinking about how I'd had no say in any of this. No voice to decline this arrangement. It was business and I was the strategic play to ensure my family stayed safe. With a reluctant exhale, I looked out at our estate one last time and fought the overwhelming pressure behind my eyes at the thought that this might be the last time I saw it or my family.

Chapter Three

TYSON

The bitch had packed too much, and I let out a barrage of expletives as I tossed her suitcases to Breck and my other man before taking the last one. There we were, three massive men carrying bright pink suitcases down the hall. I was glad Mason wasn't there with me, or I would never have heard the end of it.

Angie Donelli was going to be the death of me. There was no way I could go without killing her. Just being close to her in that room had me even more tense than Tirenti and his scumbag son. I'd forced myself to kiss her, knowing Tirenti needed proof. The way she'd gone limp in my arms, her body flush against mine, her hand clenching my jacket had left me unsettled. I wasn't sure what to make of it or the pink hue that had filled her cheeks. Her brown eyes had been wide and as inviting as her mouth had been.

Shit, I didn't know what I was thinking. I threw the bag in the trunk and removed my jacket, throwing it into the car and hearing Angie complain about hitting her with it. Rolling my sleeves up, I got in, letting Breck close my door.

Not bothering to look at her, I said, "Shut up, Angie."

From my periphery, I saw her turn back to looking out the

window. It was strange that she hadn't snapped back. She was usually quick with a comeback or a snide remark about me. But this time, she stayed quiet. After a few minutes, I glanced over at her, seeing her bring her hand up, her knuckles wiping below her eyes in a subtle move meant for me not to see.

The venom in me soothed. She was crying, something I'd never seen her do unless she was crying crocodile tears to her father to get something from him. All I'd ever seen from her was nastiness aimed at me or Casey. What she said to Casey was usually passive aggressive, side-remarks about her weight or some other comment to make her feel inferior. It never worked. My sister was too confident to let someone like Angie bring her down. But it pissed me off even more than her presence already did.

She brought her knuckles up again, wiping another tear away, and I wasn't sure what to do. Turning forward, I realized this was likely the first time she'd been away from home. Her father and brother were her life, the only life she knew, just like Armina was. And I was taking her from everything she loved and knew. Under normal circumstances, I would have called her tears out, made her feel bad for being a baby, but I remained silent, choosing to pretend I didn't notice and watching the road pass by.

When we arrived at the hangar, I waited for the guys to inspect for any sign of danger. After the incident with the Bad Omen, we took no chances. And as pissed as Tirenti was, I wouldn't put it past him to do something stupid. I was sure Mason hadn't thought this through, and Mason thought everything through. If he had, he'd have anticipated Tirenti's reaction, the slight he would experience at having me step in line for Angie and knock his son out of the running. My fist to Joey's face hadn't helped the situation.

"Come on, little Viper. Time to show you the real world," I said, stepping out of the car. I didn't know why I'd enhanced the nickname, but I liked the way it sounded when I said it, although the usual vehemence with which it left my mouth no longer accompanied it.

"I don't need to see any more of the world than Armina," she said, the tears no longer evident as she strode past me with her nose in the air. "And I have no desire to see your tiny shithole of a province."

Gritting my teeth, I bit back the urge to throw her over my knee and give her a good spanking. Just when I'd felt sorry for her, she went and returned to her usual snarky ways.

"Too bad, because my tiny shithole is where you're stuck now unless you want me to drop you off at Joey Tirenti's house. I'm sure he'd beat that attitude right out of you and have you begging like a dog for his cock in no time."

She stopped suddenly and turned to me, throwing me off guard so that I slammed into her. "You are a mean and nasty brute, Tyson Raines." She poked me in the chest with her finger on each word.

Laughing in her face, I grabbed her finger and licked it, watching the horror that overtook her features.

"Doesn't taste like pussy yet, but a few days of keeping your legs closed for other men and I bet those fingers will taste good." Her face morphed into disgust. "Although with as vile of a bitch as you are, Angie, they won't."

She snatched her hand from me and huffed away, dropping into my seat. Breck laughed behind me, and I peered over my shoulder at him. "Do you see that?" I asked as the plane door closed.

"Sure do, boss."

"You're in my seat," I told her. "Get up."

Crossing her arms, she pouted her lips at me, saying, "You have assigned seats like a schoolboy?"

My jaw ticked, my hands wringing the way I wanted to wring her neck. Walking over to her, I bent and picked her up, throwing her over my shoulder. She kicked and yelled for me to put her down, her fists hitting my back. I smacked her ass, her indignant yelp her only response. Plopping her two seats behind me, I left her there.

"Stay there or I'll tie you into the seat," I muttered, taking my seat as my men took theirs.

The flight attendant gave me a playful smile, and I considered inviting her over to put it to use, but Mason had warned me about playing with the staff. Not that I ever paid attention to him. She wasn't worth the rise I'd get out of Angie for it. I'd fucked her on my way to Armina before the shit with Donelli went down and I'd had better. Besides, Angie had me so pissed off and worked up, I wasn't sure my body could even function right now.

She walked toward me and bent down, her ample chest tempting me. "Do you need help getting settled in, Mr. Raines?"

Damn, it was tempting. "And how would you propose to help me?" I asked.

She licked her lips and my cock sprung to life, just when I'd doubted it could.

"That would do the trick," I said, about to yank those plump red lips lower.

"I don't think so," Angie said, pushing my treat away from me and sitting in the seat across from me. Her brown eyes were dark with envy. "Get your mouth away from my husband's cock and your hands off of him."

I raised a brow, trying to determine if I was angry that she'd stopped my fun or amused at her reaction.

The flight attendant looked between us, and I shrugged. "Sorry, sugar, looks like my bitch is calling the shots today."

Angie's brows creased, her mouth pursing, and I could see her gearing up with a verbal lashing.

I squeezed the flight attendant's ass, saying, "Next time," before shooing her away.

"I don't get to play, you don't get to play," Angie said.

I leaned forward. "So are you going to satisfy this hard-on?"

She jerked back, her lips parting, and I momentarily wondered if she was the kind who swallowed before I shook the thought off, becoming slightly nauseous from it.

"No. You're stuck with it, and I hope you have blue balls the whole trip." One of the guys chuckled, and I eyed them. "Hitting on that slut right in front of me," she continued to grumble.

"I wasn't hitting on her. I was taking her up on her offer and that mouth would have relieved the tension you've caused in me."

"Go to the bathroom and use your hand."

"Haven't had to do that in years, little viper. There are too many women willing to satisfy me to worry about my hand."

Her brow rose, a smirk forming. "It's gonna be a long few weeks then, Tyson, because your dick isn't getting anywhere near me and that flight attendant isn't getting within an inch of you, if I have any say."

There was something about the possessive way she made that statement that simmered in my belly. She looked out the window, her blonde hair slipping over her shoulder, and I noted the way certain streaks looked almost white as if her hours in the sun had bleached them. I'd never taken the time to really look at her, unless it was with disgust. She had a pretty face with a small nose that, when she didn't have it turned upwards, was cute. Her lips were naturally plump, the pink of her lipstick still staining them. She wore too much makeup, and I wondered what she was trying to cover up.

She turned to me, and I looked away quickly, not wanting her to see that I'd been staring and not knowing why I had been. I reminded myself how much I hated her and how annoying she was, the thoughts of her face and hair slipping below the other emotions.

Taking my phone out, I shot Mason a text to let him know just how much he owed me, adding in a warning to get his hands off my sister. A warning I knew he wouldn't heed. Angie continued to stare out the window, ignoring me. Taking the small blessing, I slid down in my seat and closed my eyes, knowing the trip was a long one and with no entertainment, there was nothing better to do.

MY EYES blinked open just as the plane began to descend. With a yawn, I glanced around, making sure my men hadn't dozed off before peeking over at Angie. She'd fallen asleep, her head leaning on the window, her mouth open slightly. She had curled her legs under her, and had her arms folded in her lap. There was a quiet innocence to her like that, one that juxtaposed the bitch she normally was. The strap of her tank top had fallen to reveal a bright pink bra, the swell of her breast spilling over it. I shook my head. Of course, it was pink. I didn't think she owned anything that wasn't pink.

"Did you still need that help, Mr. Raines?" the flight attendant asked, her seductive voice drawing my focus from the sleeping monster.

She was leaning over me, her chest sticking out again and for just a split moment I thought Angie's looked more tempting and natural.

"Nah, I'm good. Besides, you heard the lady. I'm off limits for the time being."

Her smile dropped to a frown before she sauntered away. I wiped my hand down my face, wondering what had come over me that I'd taken Angie's command and turned down what might have been a decent blowjob.

"Fuck," I muttered, my eyes meeting Angie's.

She studied me as she fluffed her hair and fixed her strap.

"You owe me a blowjob. I hope that mouth is just as good at swallowing as it is at spewing vile come-backs."

Her face morphed to disgust again. It was a look I enjoyed more and more.

"I told you, your dick isn't getting anywhere near me."

"Yet most of the men in Armina have wet their cocks in you. I think you need to re-evaluate your standards, baby."

The way her nostrils flared was perfect. I wasn't sure why I found it so amusing to piss her off, but it was certainly calming the lower half of my body, which was still aching from the loss of satisfaction.

"You're a male whore, Tyson, so you have no place to call me out on my behavior."

"That the best you can do, Angie? You're better than that." And she was. I'd been waiting for some comment about my background, about how she assumed Mason and I had grown up poor, which neither of us had. We weren't rich like we were now, but we hadn't struggled.

"You've got me off my game."

"Ha!" I stood, hearing the plane door open, and leaned over her seat. "You don't have a game. You're child's play. A bratty, little spoiled child who's trying to play with the big boys. And now about to live in a man's world. Because those boys you've been spreading your legs for are nothing compared to me."

She grabbed a fist of my shirt and yanked me closer to her. Excitement flickered in her brown eyes. "I hope you don't expect me to spread my legs for you, husband." The way she spoke the word caused a reaction in my pants that I didn't appreciate. "Because I don't play with dogs and you're the mangiest dog there is. Flea ridden, desperate, and—"

"Feral," I finished for her. "And you don't want to find out how aggressive this animal can be, because I can guarantee you won't survive."

I removed her hand from my shirt and grabbed my jacket, tossing it to her. "Cover that exposed skin up. We're not in

Armina anymore and it may be spring here, but you'll freeze those tits off if you walk off this plane like that."

Breck threw me a confused look as I walked by and exited the plane. I wasn't sure why I cared if she froze or why, after she'd called me a mangy dog, I'd given her my jacket. I heard her grousing behind me and just to piss her off, I grabbed the flight attendant and kissed her. Angie's reaction was precious, like a toddler throwing a tantrum.

I let the woman go, enjoying the breathless teeter she made as I walked away. "Maybe next time I'll take you up on that offer." I wasn't sure I really would unless Angie had me worked up, or I was desperate. She hadn't been all that good, and I'd rushed it just to shut her fake porn moans up. But maybe with her mouth full, I'd enjoy it more.

Angie smacked the back of my head, and I turned on her, grabbing her arms and shoving her against the car.

"Screw you, Tyson. Your rules remember."

"I play by my own rules, and if you ever raise your hand to me again, I'll use it to jerk me off." I shoved her harder, pinning my body against hers and not liking how it reacted.

"I hate you," she hissed.

"Good, because I despise you and I'm really questioning why I didn't hand you over to Joey Tirenti when I had the chance."

She spit in my face, and I raised my hand to hit her, seeing the fear that crossed her eyes before she masked it. I clenched my fist, fighting the urge to follow through with my instinct and leave a stinging handprint on her face. But I didn't hit women unless it was for play, no matter how bitchy they were. I pushed away from her, wiping my face and snatching the jacket from her hands.

"You can freeze. You're an icy bitch, so it shouldn't affect you."

Sitting in the front seat and ignoring Breck's grumble about having to sit with her, I stared ahead, my anger boiling over to the point that I knew I'd need a few rounds with the punching bag when we made it home. Angie huffed in the back, griping about the cold, the ride, the plane, really anything she could come up with. If complaining were a competition, she'd win the gold medal.

"Do you ever shut up?" I asked, glancing back at her.

Her eyes narrowed, and she crossed her arms before she ignored me and looked out the window.

"Huh, apparently you do." I turned back around, the heel of her sandal hitting my shoulder before it flopped on the floor in front of me. Glaring back at her, my blood pressure rose. "Don't be a cunt."

"Fuck you."

"I thought we established I would do no such thing. And I thought I warned you not to hit me again." The anger was so intense I was seeing red and I knew if a seatbelt wasn't holding me in, I'd have jumped into the back seat and strangled her.

"I didn't hit you," she replied, tipping her head up. "My shoe did."

Breck tried to stifle his laugh, but he failed, and I shot him a look. "Don't make me lock you in the same room with her all night, Breck," I warned.

His smile faltered, and I saw the horror in his eyes. Even my henchmen didn't want to be alone with her. Turning back around, I tried to calm my breathing, thanking Mason for building the airstrip close to the house.

The ride, although quick, seemed like hours. Angie muttered under her breath the rest of the way, cursing me through most of it. When we pulled through the gates, she went quiet and I knew it wasn't from the sight. The Donelli estate was just as massive as ours, so I could only assume it was reality finally settling in for her. She was in our territory now, a temporary part of our family and for someone as sheltered as she was, that was a lot to take in.

In true Angie style, she didn't stay quiet for long. On her first step from the car, the complaints started.

"This is where you live? In the boring country? Where are the clubs? The nightlife? The people?"

"Far enough away for you to keep your legs closed," I mumbled, trying to ignore the goosebumps on her skin. Night had fallen and although the days were warm, the nights were still chilly. She was trying her best not to let it show that she was cold, balling her hands into fists and clamping her mouth shut...until she started complaining again.

"This is a nightmare. I hate the country. Do you even have a pool? Why is there gravel under my shoes?"

I rolled my eyes and pushed past her, walking into the house and considering if closing the door on her was an option. Mason and Casey were in the kitchen, and Mason hadn't heeded my warning. He had Casey on the counter, his hands on her ass as they kissed.

"Dammit, Mace. I told you to keep your hands off her," I grumbled.

"Not gonna happen. She's too sexy not to touch," he replied, giving her another kiss before helping her hop down.

"Casey!" Angie yelled, running over to her and hugging her. Mason and I looked at each other, his eyes questioning if this was normal. Which it wasn't. But then again, none of this was normal for Angie, and Casey was part of her life at home.

"Hey, Anj," she replied, freeing herself from Angie's hold and shooting me the same confused look Mason had given me.

I shrugged, having had enough of Angie to last a lifetime and really needing to get away from her.

"Have you lost weight?" Angie asked. "Your ass doesn't look as big."

If Angie was smart, she'd have noticed the daggers coming from Casey's eyes and mine. But Casey didn't need protecting. She was good at giving it right back and would have if Mason hadn't spoken up first.

"I hope not," he said. "I like that ass plump." He gave Casey a smack on her ass, and she jumped with a giggle.

I had to hand it to Mason. Even if I was still uncomfortable with their relationship, he loved my sister, everything about her, and he made her happy. As long as Casey was happy, I was happy. And there was no question that he was head over heels for her. I'd never seen him adore someone like he adored my sister.

"So you two are still a thing?" Angie said, acting like she hadn't just insulted my sister, and Mason hadn't just affirmed that they were. She moved closer to him, her hand ready to touch when Casey slid between them.

"Mine, Angie. You have your own." She nodded to me, and I wanted to put her in a headlock like I used to when we were little. "Right, Ty?"

I grimaced, crossing my arms and hoping she could read the irritation in my eyes.

"Looks like the honeymoon is going well," Mason joked, rubbing salt into the wound.

"Something like that. Casey, can you pick a room out for the bitch? I'm going to get changed and take some of my anger out on the punching bag instead of her face."

I stormed out, but stopped in my tracks as Mason said, "Not so fast. You need to pack. Donelli called me while you were in flight. Tirenti's not backing down, so your acting skills need improvement. You leave for the island in the morning."

My teeth were grinding so hard I could hear them. "And why would I do that?"

"Because you and your new wife are honeymooning there."

Chapter Four

ANGIE

T he nightmare just kept getting worse. Tyson stomped away as my jaw dropped. A honeymoon? This couldn't be happening. None of this could be.

"Come on, I'll show you to your room," Casey said.

Mason grabbed her as she walked by and pulled her in for a kiss. I could see by the way her entire body leaned into his that it was a sensual one. I wanted to be happy for her, but I was stuck in this mess and there was a part of me that was jealous. There was no way I would ever admit that to anyone. While I enjoyed partying and the sex that came with it, I'd never had a man kiss me like that. They'd only ever kissed me with the intention of having sex with me, which was exactly how I liked it. No commitment, no intimacy, no ability to see me for anything more than what I presented to them. The sexy, self-assured, rich daughter of the man who held the power in our territory.

Mason let her go, and a deep blush filled her cheeks.

"Don't dawdle, princess," he said in a low voice that would have had any woman swooning. "I plan to finish what I started before these two interrupted us."

Damn, he was hot. He wasn't my usual type, but there was no

denying his sex appeal. Why did I have to get stuck with Tyson? The asshole who was nothing but mean to me, who only looked at me with disgust. Not that I wanted him to look at me any other way, but he may have been just as sexy if he did. I thought about that moment when I'd caught him looking at me on the plane. It was an unguarded moment, and I'd noticed how the gold specks in his eyes had shimmered with something almost sweet. His thick brown curls were messy from sleep, giving him a cute, boyish look. But it had faded, the hard glares returning along with the insults.

I wanted to make a snide comment about how I could help Mason finish, but I didn't have the energy. Being with Tyson all day had drained me and the thought of crawling into bed and sleeping was too inviting. Following Casey through the house, I tried not to think about my father or how much I missed him and Tony. This place was so different from ours, this territory so cold and far from the beach. At least we'd be out of here in the morning, heading to the island. I wasn't sure what island, but it didn't matter. As long as there was sun and sand, I'd be happy.

"You'll stay in this room," Casey said, stopping in front of a door. She sounded a little too giddy, especially when she followed it up with, "Good luck getting any sleep."

She walked off with too much pep in her step, and I didn't think it had anything to do with the man waiting for her in the kitchen.

"What about my bags?" I asked.

"Get them yourself. We're self-sufficient around here, Angie. That spoiled girl shit doesn't fly in this province."

She was around the corner before I could think of something smart to say back. Damn. I'd have to find my way back to the front of the house and I hadn't paid any attention to where she'd taken me. With a huff, I opened the door.

"What the fuck?" Tyson snapped.

He was pulling a t-shirt over his head, covering a sexy chest lined with muscles and tattoos. I couldn't think of anything to say, my eyes following the material of the shirt as it covered his stomach, then tracking his solid arms and the tattoos that decorated them. Swallowing, I glanced up at his face. He wore a smirk that normally would have irritated the shit out of me, but for some horrid reason, sent a surge of warmth through my lower body. His eyes danced with amusement.

"I thought I told you my dick was off limits, little viper." Shit, the way he said that nickname held a different tone, and that warmth became a burning.

I needed to pull myself together. This was Tyson Raines, not some hunk I wanted to touch or even look at, despite how good he looked in those gray sweatpants and that black t-shirt.

"Keep it in your pants, asshole." My words didn't carry the same acidity they usually did, and I worried that he'd notice.

"Believe me, I will. Now get out of my room." There he was. The harsh prick had returned, the smirk overtaken by a frown.

"This is where Casey said I was sleeping, so get out of *my* room."

"Unfucking believable. There's no way I'm sharing my room with you. All the rooms in this house and they think...I'm gonna kill Mason and don't even get me started on what I'm gonna do to Casey."

He stomped to the door and, with a shrug, I sat on his bed. "Do I want to know how many times you've jerked off in these sheets?" I asked, gingerly picking up the corner of his comforter.

He swiveled to me, walking over and yanking me off the bed. The force sent me into his chest, which I didn't think was his intention because he froze just like I did. It was a strangely comfortable place to be, and I inadvertently leaned further into it, noticing the distinct bulge in his pants and how enticingly large it was.

"I thought you didn't want to play with me?" I said, flicking my eyes downward and knowing how pissed he'd be that I'd noticed.

He shoved me back, and I landed hard on the bed, the fall knocking the wind from me. The breath I'd been taking stuck as he dropped over me and hovered just close enough to stir something in me that I didn't like.

"I can guarantee I don't want to play with your bratty, used body. And no, I don't need to jerk off in my bed. I have plenty of women to choose from and any stains you find are from the last one I had in it."

"You don't use protection?" I asked, tilting my head and trying not to let him see the effect he was having on me, the one I was cursing because I hated this man with a passion.

My question threw him off and his brow creased like he didn't know how to answer it.

"You do?" he asked, his tone curious.

"Of course, idiot. If they're having sex with me one night, they're doing the same with other women another night, and... ewww."

He laughed, the tension fading, but he was still hovering over me. "You never let them go bare?"

"I..." I never had. I was on the pill for extra protection, but I had never been that attached to anyone, nor did I trust anyone enough to let them come inside of me. I wasn't about to tell Tyson that, though. "No, it's gross."

He laughed even harder, and I hit his chest.

"Don't laugh. With all the sluts you sleep with, you're a prime example of why I don't want that shit inside of me."

His eyes hardened. "I use protection, bitch."

My hand hadn't removed from his chest when I'd hit him. It was still hanging there, the firm muscles below tense again. He glanced down at it, then back at me.

"All the time?" I asked, not really knowing why, but Tyson was like me in more ways than I wanted to admit. Both of us seeking something in the casual hook-ups we regularly had. That thought hit me hard because I knew it was the truth, even if we hated each other.

He lifted himself from me and rolled his neck, giving me a look I couldn't read as I leaned up on my elbows.

"Most of the time, unless it's serious."

"And has it ever been serious?" What was wrong with me? I didn't care, just like he didn't.

His eyes scrunched, like he was trying to figure out the same thing. "Not in a very long time. Now get out of my bed and my room. I expect you to be gone when I get back or I'll call that flight attendant up and have her blow me in front of you."

He grabbed his phone and left, slamming the door behind him. Dropping back onto the bed, I stared at the ceiling, wondering why I'd asked those questions and why my heart had raced when he'd been hovering over me. Deciding that aggravating him again would make me feel better, I sat up and looked around the room. It was messy, but no more messy than my brother's room. Rising, I walked, my fingers draping over the personal life of a man I'd never been close to, never caring who he was because he pissed me off so much. Small insights into the man he was. A framed picture of him with Casey when they were younger sat on his dresser. I picked it up, only then realizing how much older he was than me. Casey was a few years older than me, but Tyson was in his mid-thirties.

Chewing my lip, I set the frame down and picked up another picture. It was of a couple who looked blissful and in love. The woman was looking up at the man, her smile large as his hazel eyes looked back at her. Her long brown curls matched Casey's and the mop of curls on Tyson's head. Their parents. I'd never bothered going to Casey's apartment, never caring what her life was outside of our family even when I'd dragged her shopping or clubbing with me. I knew their parents were dead, but that was all. I'd never asked about them or really much of anything that didn't pertain to me.

Replacing the photo, I shoved away the guilt that threatened to settle on my shoulders. I didn't want to care about their life outside of me and my world. Nothing mattered but me and what made me happy. I fortified myself with those thoughts, knowing they were the same ones that had driven me for years and shaped me into the woman who Tyson detested, the one most people hated unless they were having sex with me.

Throwing my shoulders back and holding my head high, I trudged out of the room, determined to find my luggage and another room to sleep in. But I didn't know this house and the further I got from Tyson's room, the lonelier I felt and the more my homesickness hit. Turning around, I gave up on my search for my luggage and returned to his room.

After using the bathroom and finding it surprisingly clean, I walked into Tyson's closet, thinking I'd grab a sweatshirt or something to keep the chill away that had seeped into my bones. My hand drifted over suit jackets and button downs. A variety of ties hung neatly in the back, where a small dresser sat. One drawer was open, and I pulled out the handful of dark silk scarves that seemed so oddly feminine among the rest of the masculine room. I would have questioned who they belonged to, but they were on top of more family photos and a small jewelry box with the name Lilly Raines engraved on it. I dropped the scarves but a blue one slipped free, landing on the closet floor.

I picked it up, rubbing the smooth material through my fingers as I contemplated why I'd thought wearing something of Tyson's made any sense. No matter how cold I was, I didn't want something of his on me.

I crawled into his bed, trying to forget his comments about stains and finding the smell of him that lingered on the sheets surprisingly comforting. I drifted off with thoughts of how irritated that made me, the scarf still in my hand and providing a strange sense of comfort.

THE SOUND of water running woke me and I blinked. My eyes opened just as it turned off. Shit, I'd fallen asleep in Tyson's bed. But he hadn't woken me or thrown me out, which seemed strange. Lifting my eyes, I perused the room, not seeing him and wondering why he had left me sleeping. The shower. That was him in the bathroom. Sitting up quickly, my eyes met his. He was toweling his hair dry, the muscles of his chest flexing with every move of his arm. His black pants sat low on his waist and my eyes traveled the path to where they sat on his hips. Damn, he was sexy, and I hated how easily that thought had come to me. I needed to get a grip and remember that Tyson was an asshole who treated me like I was a gnat he couldn't get away from.

But words wouldn't form, and he beat me to the punch.

"I thought I said you needed to be out of my bed and my room, or did I not make that clear last night?"

"Is that what you tell all your women? Use them and kick them out that same night?"

"Damn right it is, unless I keep them longer so they can repay me with a blow job."

I studied him, wondering how much of his macho talk was the truth. I knew he slept around because he did it when he visited my father, too, but he talked it up with harsh words and a bravado that made me think he was talking a bigger game. Or maybe he wasn't, and he said things like that to cover the true reason he was such a playboy. The same reason I searched men out...to make me feel something other than the loneliness, the pain of the truth that I wanted more but didn't know how to have more. That I didn't trust any of the men I met to give me the more I craved. That the sex would dull the pain, that it would satisfy the hunger that sat below the surface.

"Repay you for what? For letting you fuck them?" I asked.

He walked into his closet, and I took in his muscular back, the power of it, of him. There was nothing about Tyson Raines that was like any man I'd ever been with, and I shook off the curiosity of what those muscles would feel like against my body. He came back out, buttoning up the dress shirt he now wore.

"For giving them the best orgasm of their life and then letting me fuck them."

Now it was my turn to laugh. "I doubt that," I said, running my fingers through my hair to untangle the knots.

He narrowed his eyes at me. "I doubt you've ever come as hard as I could make you come, little viper."

My inhale was louder than it should have been, and the way my panties grew soaked left me completely out of sorts. Shit, I was out of control and I didn't like it. I hated Tyson, and I needed to remember that.

Standing, I tossed my hair over my shoulder, suddenly conscious of the fact that I had morning breath, messy hair, and my makeup was likely smudged.

"And I doubt you've ever had a woman make you come as hard as I could make you come, Raines," I said, giving him a sly smile before walking past him and into the bathroom, making sure my ass was swaying in a perfect rhythm.

He snorted, and I glanced over my shoulder at him. His eyes were dark and for a moment, they held a flicker of desire that he covered quickly. "Get out of my bathroom."

"I need to shower. Be a good husband and get my bags."

I slammed the bathroom door, hearing his grumbled swearing and complaining. That was better. The aggression between us was a comfort I embraced. The other emotions were ones I didn't understand and ones that completely unsettled me.

I made do with the bathroom products he had, wishing I'd

taken the time to take my face cleanser and expensive shampoo out of my bag. I used his razer to touch up my legs. If we were going to an island, I wanted to be smooth. I had my other parts waxed regularly, but there was something soothing about shaving my legs, so I'd never included them in my waxing routine.

Finding a spare towel in the small closet in the bathroom, I wrapped it around myself and stepped from the bathroom, intent on grabbing my lotion, face cream, and makeup from my bags. My contacts were so dry my eyes were uncomfortable, and I really needed to switch my pair out.

To my surprise, he'd brought my bags in. I'd expected to have to wander the house to find them and the move seemed like a sweet one...until I saw him leaning against the door, his arms crossed as his eyes perused my bare skin.

"It's nothing more than you usually see, Tyson," I said, searching through a case for some clothes.

He walked over to me and grabbed my shoulders, turning me to him. His eyes were soft, and he brushed a thumb across my nose and over my cheek. My heart thumped, remembering my makeup wasn't on.

"You have freckles," he murmured.

I tried to turn away, but he held my chin, forcing my eyes to his.

"I hate them," I admitted, dropping my eyes. No one knew I had them or the birthmark on the edge of my cheek he hadn't noticed. I covered them up with makeup, ensuring no one saw them. They were like a blemish I couldn't get rid of.

"They're cute," he said in a sweet tone that made my heart leap in a way I didn't like. "You should leave the makeup off."

He let me go, running his hand through his hair before saying, "Get dressed. Our plane leaves in an hour and then we're stuck with each other for a week."

"Should be fun," I said, covering up the vulnerable sensation that sat in my chest. The one that was reflected in his features. "A week of insults and jabs. Maybe you can come up with some new ones since you use bitch and cunt so frequently."

That smirk returned and the way it slithered into my body and warmed it left me confused.

"I'm sure I can think of a few more."

He walked away, leaving me alone, and I stared at the door, struggling with the emotions battling within me. I wanted to scream and throw something at the door. He drove me mad, and how I was suddenly reacting to him was driving me even crazier.

I hate him, I hate him, I hate him. The mantra repeated through my head as I dressed. Taking my makeup bag into the bathroom, I glanced in the mirror, taking in the freckles I hid, ones the boys had teased me relentlessly about when I was little. The same ones I'd traced the pattern of on my mother's face when I was small, before she'd grown ill, before death had ripped her from us. I had loved her freckles, how her brown eyes had smiled when my tiny hands had traced patterns in them. But I'd never loved my own, especially after her death.

I looked away, pulling out my makeup and covering the signs of my vulnerability, of who I really was, preferring to be the spoiled brat Tyson thought I was. That everyone thought I was. I peeled my contacts out, replacing them, thankful he hadn't noticed those. That was the last thing I needed, and I could only imagine the teasing names he'd relentlessly call me if he ever found the glasses I hid at the bottom of my bag for emergency.

Checking myself over and ensuring I looked suitably sexy and expensive, I sealed up my suitcase and wandered through the house, eventually finding my way back to the large living room that led to the kitchen. Tyson was leaning against the counter, his arms crossed, an unhappy frown on his face. Casey was yapping about something while Mason eyed her, his eyes hungry.

"Didn't you just have sex with her?" I asked him. Tyson's glare fell on me, but I ignored it, checking my manicure instead.

"Eh, that was two hours ago," Mason replied with a shrug. "I'm ready for more."

"Must not have satisfied him," I quipped, earning a nasty look from Casey.

"Just because you don't know how to please a man with that skinny body of yours, don't assume I don't. He craves me because I'm like a drug he can't get enough of," she snapped right back.

Mason rose and pulled her into his arms, kissing her so hard she dropped the plate she was holding.

"Would you two stop that?" Tyson grouched.

"What do you think, princess? Should we stop?"

She giggled and returned to kissing him.

"Fuck, you two are killing me." Tyson turned back to me. "Let's go."

"But breakfast—"

He snatched my arm and dragged me from the room. "No breakfast. You took your time sleeping in and getting ready, and now we're late."

"Have fun, you guys!" Casey shouted from the doorway as he continued to drag me.

"I'll have fun when I'm strangling her," Tyson mumbled.

"She might like that, Ty," Mason joked.

"Get your hands off me, you big brute." I smacked at him until he let me go faster than I thought he would and I lost my balance. Falling hard, my ankle turned slightly in my heels before my ass hit the floor. I winced but bit back the cry as pain flared through it.

Tyson loomed over me, a look of concern crossing his face until I said, "You're such an asshole. I'd take Joey's slimy hands over yours any day."

Face contorting, his jaw went rigid. The hazel in his eyes was so dark they were almost brown. "Get up and stop playing the dumb spoiled girl card. It's not sexy and the only reason anyone pays attention to you is because you whore yourself out and throw your daddy's money around. I'm not falling for it and I'm not picking your stupid ass up."

He stormed off, his words stinging as much as the throbbing in my ankle. I'd never felt so small, so seen as I did then. Knowing Casey and Mason were watching, I huffed a breath to blow my hair from my face, yelling, "Just because the only way you can get a woman on her back is to drop her doesn't mean that will work on me, prick."

He stopped, his hand on the doorknob, the chilly air blowing in and reminding me that I had no clothes for this province. The air cut right through my thin dress.

I shoved the skirt lower as he snarled, "I prefer my women on their knees and knowing how snobby you and your preppy trust-fund pups are, I can guarantee they've never put that mouth to use like it should be which is why it does nothing but spew childish insults. Get up and get in the car before I take you to Joey and let him bruise those delicate knees."

He threw the door open the rest of the way, the wind picking my skirt up and tossing it up to reveal my underwear. I heard him order one of his men to get my bags as I pulled it down. Glancing over, I noticed Casey and Mason had left us alone, and I wondered how much they'd heard and seen. With a sigh, I pushed up from the ground, gritting my teeth at the pain in my ankle but walking on it anyway. I made it to the car, flopping into the seat with an *oof*, relieved to be off it and hoping I could keep from crying because it was aching more. I wasn't certain if the pressure behind my eyes was from my ankle, Tyson's words, or how miserable this situation was. Whatever the reason, I bit my lip and stared out the window, glad he'd taken the front seat so I didn't have to put up with him so close to me.

Chapter Five

TYSON

Running my hands down my face, I climbed into the front seat. Angie was driving me mad. Everything she did grated on my nerves and every comment from her mouth shredded them further. But there were moments when there was something about her that drew me to her. Like the way we'd spoken so easily about our sex lives, as if we talked like that all the time. Or the way she'd slept in my bed, curled up and innocent, seeming so small in my enormous bed, my mother's scarf clutched in her hand. That she'd gone through my things had given me the urge to wake her and force her out, but something stopped me, that part of me that liked how vulnerable she seemed in that moment, that liked the freckles across her nose and cheeks, that enjoyed the way her eyes had greedily perused my chest before she'd caught herself. And that was bothering me like a bite that wouldn't stop itching.

I didn't know what was wrong with me or why she was having this effect on me. I hadn't meant for her to fall. Hearing her ass hit the floor so hard had me cringing, but then she'd snapped back at me and the feeling had disappeared, the hatred returning. She was such a brat; I wanted to wrap my hands around her neck and snap it. I flexed my fingers, remembering how her eyes had lit when I'd brought my hand up her neck in Armina. She said she liked it rough, but I knew the type of men she let near her, the ones her father's men vetted. The rich and image conscious who would never dare touch the daughter of Vince Donelli in any way she didn't invite. And Angie wasn't the kind to invite aggression, to want a man like me to take her, because no matter how easy she was or how experienced she made herself out to be, she couldn't handle someone like me. She'd break too easily.

Raking my fingers through my hair, I questioned why I was thinking of breaking her, of being the one to test just how delicate she was. I needed to remember that she'd insulted me at every turn, that mouth never failing to put me down, those brown eyes flicking at me dismissively every time I saw her.

The irritation returned, my prior thoughts fleeing as we drew closer to the hangar. By the time I took my seat in the plane, watching her walk to a seat behind me, her head held high, nose in the air, and eyes avoiding me, the hatred had returned. I half wished I hadn't told Mason to cancel the flight attendant just to annoy Angie more, but I'd had a touch of softness after our moment in the bedroom. One I was regretting as she sat silently behind me, just as she had in the car. What was wrong with her? She never stayed this quiet for more than a few seconds.

I glanced back at her as the plane pulled out of the hangar. She was looking out the window, biting her lip, her arms wrapped tight around her. Only then did I realize she wore another of those flimsy dresses she wore in Armina. She had to be freezing. Even though the weather was fine to me, she wasn't used to our climate. I turned around, dropping my head against the seat. I had been hard on her at the house, and I'd seen the hurt in her eyes. We were always nasty to each other, but I'd hit low, and I could tell it had affected her. Not that I cared, because I didn't.

The plane took off, and I motioned for Finch to get me a drink.

"A little early, isn't it, boss?" he asked.

"No sexy flight attendant to occupy me this time, Finch. Besides, with that one on board, I need a few stiff drinks to survive."

I waited for her to reply with some witty retort, anything to knock me down a level, but nothing came. I peeked back at her. She hadn't moved. Finch fixed me a drink, and I motioned to her with my head. He shrugged and returned to his seat. With a sigh, I took a swig of the scotch and let it go, thinking I'd take the silence as a gift from her usual annoying mouth and hating that I suddenly missed it.

THE FLIGHT to the island was a few hours and Angie stayed quiet the entire time. When we landed, my men disembarked first, scouting the area out, one heading to the resort to ensure there were no unexpected visitors. Mason owned the island and had built a luxury resort on it, one that housed only a handful of guests. The richest of the rich who paid a hefty price for the privacy. We wouldn't be alone, but the resort manager knew to pass every guest through Mason and me, so whoever was here would be discreet and no threat to me or Angie.

Regardless, I waited for Finch to return, glancing back at Angie, who still hadn't moved. Damn it. I rose and walked to her, pushing her legs aside and sitting in front of her. Leaning forward, I waited for her to say something smartassed. She was biting her lip so hard she'd broken the skin, and I nudged her foot with mine. The cry she tried to stifle clawed at me in a way I didn't like, and I reached over and forced her to look at me. Her brown eyes were watery, the tears pushing to fall.

"Anj?"

"Go to hell, Tyson."

I let her go, remembering how the cry had come after I'd hit her foot. I grabbed her leg and pulled her foot into my lap, her yelp confirming I'd found the culprit. Gingerly, I ran my fingers over her ankle, which was puffy.

"Why didn't you say something?" I asked, looking back up at her.

"You would have laughed at me," she said, trying to pull her leg from my hold.

"Did you do this when you fell?"

She looked away, and I realized she had. And I'd been the reason, making her fall when I'd been rough with her. My anger had caused this, and a wave of guilt pummeled through me.

"We've got the okay to move, boss," Finch said, peeking his head in.

"Do you still have that first-aid kit on board?" I asked him.

"Sure do." He made some noise as he shuffled through things to find it, but I didn't take my eyes from Angie, who was questioning me with hers.

"It's fine, Tyson," she said.

"No, it's not. It's swollen." I took her shoe off, trying to ignore how soft and delicate her skin was. Delicate. That's what I'd called her while I'd insulted her, right after I'd basically called her a whore who men used for her body and her father's money. She was right, I was an ass.

Finch handed me a bandage, and I wrapped it around Angie's foot, ignoring her protests. When her ankle was secure, I picked her other leg up and pulled her heel off, handing it and the other to Finch. Gingerly lowering her feet, I stood, grabbing her arm as she tried to stand.

"I don't think so, little viper." Not giving her time to reply, I scooped her up and carried her from the plane. She was so light it barely seemed like she was in my arms, but having her there felt oddly right.

"Tyson, put me down. This is ridiculous. Do you do this to all your women? You drop them on their ass as an excuse to carry them to your room? Or maybe you just have to carry them there to force them to have sex with you?" Her attempt to insult me was half-hearted, so I let it go.

"Are you saying you're one of my women?" I asked, raising my brow as I lowered her into the waiting car.

Her eyes searched mine, and for just that moment, I had the urge to kiss her. It was a crazy thought, one that had to be from the situation, or maybe the island air.

"I am your *wife*," she teased, giving me a flirty smile, one that erased all the harsh insults that had floated on the air between us.

"So you are," I responded, brushing my thumb over her cheek and wishing her freckles were still present. "No more heels. And no more make-up, for that matter."

"But—"

I put my finger to her lips, slowly letting it slide over her bottom lip, her mouth parting with a sexy exhale. I needed to stop because a strange craving was building in me, one that was at war with how I normally felt about her. It was a hostile craving that was fighting for dominance, fighting to forget that I despised the brat who was too young, too conceited, too self-obsessed for me to even consider touching.

She narrowed her eyes, turning her face from me. Taking my seat, I leaned my head back, trying to clear my mind. The car ride was brief, the island small, so the silence that sat between us didn't fester.

"We've got the room next door and one of us will be just outside at all times," Finch said, when I exited the car.

I buttoned my jacket, glancing around the resort and noting the massive security presence already in place. We didn't take chances; the clientele was too important, and the resort was a solid revenue source we didn't want to risk losing.

"This is more like it," Angie said, causing me to turn to her.

She had left the car and was trying to walk around without

letting me see she was still in pain. My jaw tightened, and I quirked a brow at her. "And what do you think you're doing?"

"Walking into the resort so I can have a strong drink and flirt with some hot staff member."

The tick in my jaw was sharp. She was back to her old self, that strange moment between us gone, just like always, as if neither of us could deal with what a moment like that might mean.

"Not gonna happen, wife." A slight shudder went through her when I said the word.

Moving to her, I scooped her up in one quick sweep, ignoring her protests.

"I am not some object you own and can just toss around whenever you want," she griped, pressing her hand against my chest.

"I do own you, Angie. Your father sold you off to me and now I get to toss you around whenever I want. If you'd like, I can throw you over my shoulder and spank your ass instead."

That shut her up, and she pursed her lips invitingly. My reaction to the look unnerved me and I focused my eyes ahead, seeing the resort manager waiting just inside for us.

I nodded to her, saying, "Send the resort doctor up to our room."

"Yes, Mr. Raines," she replied, pushing her dark hair back as her green eyes looked seductively at me.

Angie's hand on my chest curled into a fist that was pulling my shirt so tight my collar was choking me. I continued walking, following my men to our room. When we were inside, I tossed her on the bed, but her grip on my shirt didn't loosen and I tipped over her, stopping myself with my hands around her head.

"What the fuck, Angie?"

"Did you have sex with that woman?" she hissed, and I wondered at the possessiveness in that sound.

"Does it matter?" I asked, creasing my eyes.

"Maybe. I'm supposed to be your wife. How am I supposed to play that part when that woman is flirting with you?"

"Are you jealous?" The thought lit a strange fire in me.

"No, idiot," she snapped, letting my shirt go finally.

Only then did I realize my body was against hers, the feel of it oddly comfortable. Not liking it, I lifted myself, straightening my arms so I was still above her. Glancing down, I noticed how far her dress had bunched up when we'd fallen, the curve of her hip fully exposed, the thin lacey strap of her pink panties too visible. I'd seen plenty of her body. She walked around in tiny bikinis, her normal outfits barely covering her tits and ass, but something about seeing her like this caused my pants to tent uncomfortably.

I met her eyes again.

"Did you sleep with her?" she asked almost breathlessly.

"What if I did?"

Her lips thinned, jealousy clear in her eyes this time. What was happening to us?

"No, I didn't sleep with her. I've only been here once, a few years ago with Mason when he brought Riley here. He has a strict rule which I usually disregard about touching the staff. Since Riley was with us, I was a good boy."

She relaxed, the darkness in her eyes lifting.

"But that doesn't mean I didn't play."

"Get off me, asshole. And you can keep that hard-on away from me and her."

I laughed and as I rose, my hand brushed her thigh inadvertently.

"Someone needs to satisfy it, and her mouth looked damned inviting." I removed my jacket, rolling my neck and turning to glare at her when a pillow hit my back.

A knock at the door saved her from my retaliation. Finch peeked his head in.

"She's still alive. That's impressive, boss," he joked, inciting a fury of swearing from Angie.

She stood, and I stormed over to her, pushing her back on the bed and pulling her skirt down further, some abnormal need to keep that skin from anyone's eyes driving me.

"You're an..."

The doctor walked in, followed by the resort manager, and Angie's entire demeanor changed. She pulled herself up, propping a pillow behind her. "What's she doing in here?"

"I'm sure she's just ensuring the doctor gives you the best care," I answered, not sure why she was so jealous of the woman who didn't hold a candle to her. There weren't many who did. I wiped my hand down my face, cursing myself for the thought as the doctor unwrapped her ankle and started looking at it.

I stood back, the manager stepping closer to me. Her hand touched my arm, and I looked down at it, giving her a questioning look. She'd been flirty the last time I'd been here, a bit too desperate, and I'd read her attempts as a way to advance her position or her pay. I rarely gave a damn about Mason's rule of not touching the help, but I'd heeded it with this one, only returning her flirting, a few touches here, a drunken kiss where my hands may have slid down to her firm tits. But I'd stopped the action when she'd reached for my pants. That halt had been painful, and I'd worked out the tension with a few women when I'd returned home.

"He'll be a few minutes," she said, licking her lips. "Maybe we can go work out the details of your stay."

Shit, she was bold and if Angie had been her regular self, I would have taken her up on it just to piss Angie off. Angie's head shot up.

"Ty," Angie said in a seductive voice that reached in and jerked my body the way this woman's invitation hadn't. Angie had done something to me that I couldn't shake. It was like she'd damaged me, and I didn't like it.

I turned to her as the doctor stood. She drew her other leg up, her skirt slipping further up her thigh, the doctor's eyes falling to it. I clenched my fist and jerked away from the manager, stalking over to Angie and yanking her dress over her leg, as far as the insufficient material would allow. Angie grabbed my shirt and pulled me to her lips, kissing me possessively and stirring a fire in me. Threading my fingers through her hair, I pushed her mouth further into mine. She was putting on a show, but the way she was kissing me was more than simply a way of staking her claim in front of another woman. It was a claim of ownership that seeped its way through my body. I needed to get a grip and so did she. We were enemies, two people who couldn't stand being close to each other, who had hated each other for years. Since the moment I'd met her as a snotty eighteen-year-old and through the years as she'd become a woman, a sexy, confident, demanding thing who grated on my every nerve.

Her lips parted from mine and we stared at each other for seconds that seemed to last an eternity because that kiss had differed from the others.

"Keep your hands off my husband," she said, her eyes never leaving mine, that claim clear.

Pulling myself together, I removed her hands from my shirt and smoothed down the material. The next move was mine. I could take us back to where we'd been, the comfortable hatred that sat between us, and leave the room with the other woman. Fuck my confusion out on her willing body and drive the wedge back between me and Angie. Hurt her like I normally would have. Or I could send the woman away, play the game that had turned dangerous. And not hurt her.

Her brown eyes were on mine, and in them I saw the plea. The need for me to let her win this battle, to not hurt her. Turning from her, I walked to the resort manager, bypassing the doctor who I'd deal with momentarily. Expectation sat in the woman's eyes, and I heard the disappointed sigh from Angie as I reached my hand into the woman's hair and pulled her closer to me. Her lips parted, and the emotion rolling from Angie in waves added to the silence that had encompassed the room.

"You heard my wife," I said, tugging harder. "I'm off limits and I suggest you keep your hands and that tempting mouth to yourself, or you'll need to find another job."

Her eyes grew wide, and I released her hair, turning back to the doctor. "Tell me what's wrong with her ankle and if I catch your eyes on any part of her body but her ankle, I'll break every one of your fingers." Without taking my eyes from him, I said, "Finch, see her out while we talk."

I heard the manager grumble as Finch escorted her out. The doctor cleared his throat uncomfortably before apologizing and telling me it was only a minor twist, and she needed to rest it for a week.

"An entire week?" she asked.

"Yes," he answered. "If you don't, you'll injure it worse and then you'll be down for a month."

"Looks like I'll be carrying you everywhere, baby. Either that or we won't be leaving this room." I disliked how that thought caused a jolt in my system.

She pouted her lip out, crossing her arms and emphasizing her cleavage. Cleavage I'd purposely avoided looking at in the past, but that my eyes now sank to.

"Let me wrap it again and I'll get you some pain reliever. That should help with the swelling and the discomfort."

"Discomfort?" she said. "It hurts like a beast!"

"That's because you're wimpy, little viper. Your bark is better than your bite."

"Don't make me bite you, Tyson," she retorted.

"I invite that, baby. Anytime you want." And I wasn't sure I didn't mean it.

I walked away, squeezing the bridge of my nose as the doctor wrapped her ankle, giving her instructions to keep it iced and elevated. The balcony door was open, and I stood outside, taking in the warm air and the island view. Mason had ensured we had the best view, the beach below, the ocean stirring and never-ending beyond it. The room was large enough but there was only one bed and since Angie was stuck resting her ankle, that meant I was on the couch.

"Great," I grumbled.

"She's all set, Mr. Raines. I'll have pain reliever sent to the room. Make sure she takes it twice a day. I gave her the first dose to ease the swelling. She'll be up and about in no time. Just keep her off her feet for now."

"Thank you," I said, not bothering to look at him. I heard him leave but continued to take in the view, not wanting to deal with the one that was sitting in the bed behind me.

"Boss, we brought the luggage up. We'll be outside and next door if you need anything."

"Thanks, Finch."

He left just as my phone rang.

"Mace," I answered.

"How's life with the viper?" he teased.

"Just peachy," I said, turning to look at her. She was trying to scoot down the bed to reach the suitcases that were on the floor. Shaking my head, I continued, "The bitch twisted her ankle and now I've gotta deal with her whiny demands."

She looked sharply at me. "Fuck you, Raines."

"That and she's put a restraint on my cock. Remember that sexy resort manager?"

"Damn it, Ty. No touching the help," Mason groused.

"Simmer down. I didn't touch her. The viper put me on lockdown."

His laugh came through the phone, irritating me.

"What do you want, Mace?"

I walked over to the bed and jerked Angie back.

"Donelli called me. Tirenti's not letting up. He wants proof that you're on a honeymoon and not playing games. His son is adamant that Angie is his, and that you stole her just to piss him off."

"He's a slimy loser. He wants pictures? Probably of her tits, so he can jerk off to them," I grumbled as I tossed two of her bags on the bed. Why she needed so much luggage was beyond my comprehension.

"I'm not sending him a titty shot!" she complained, moving back down the bed. I threw her a look that stopped her in her tracks.

"Get your ass against the headboard and lift that leg."

"Did I interrupt something?" Mason asked. "I was worried I'd interrupt you murdering her, not having sex with her."

"Shut up, Mace. I'm not fucking her. I'm trying to keep her from screwing her ankle up more. She's like a damned toddler."

She started bitching again, but I ignored her, opening a suitcase and rummaging through her clothes. I picked up a tiny pink thong and held it up, raising my brow.

"Do you own anything but pink?" I asked with a shake of my head.

She crawled down the bed, a sight that gripped my balls uncomfortably, the move offering me a view straight down her dress.

"This isn't the best time, Mason. What do you need from us?" I dropped the panties and moved to the side of the bed, grabbing a handful of her hair and throwing her back down. She landed with an exhale that did nothing but make me harder, and I knew I needed to get away from her. The mix of fury and lust that was mingling in that hostility within me was dangerous.

She reached up, trying to disentangle my fingers from her hair while Mason talked, my ears not hearing anything but the annoyed cursing coming from Angie's mouth.

"I'll call you back." Hanging up, I threw the phone aside and pinned her with my other hand.

"You're a prick, Tyson."

"I am, baby, and you're the pinch to my nerves that turns me into that prick." I released her hair and grabbed her wrists, pinning them over her head as I leaned over her. "Sit still and prop that damn ankle up, or I'll tie you to the damned bed."

She hissed, and I had the urge to do it just to see what she'd look like that way.

"Shit," I muttered, releasing her and rising. She was driving me mad, and I needed to walk away. "Stay here," I said, snatching my phone from the floor and walking to the door.

"And if I don't?" she asked, her voice the snotty one I knew well.

"I'll spank you so hard you won't be able to sit comfortably for the rest of the trip." I stormed out, slamming the door behind me and ignoring Finch's grin as I dialed Mason back.

"That bad, huh?" he asked when he answered.

"She's driving me crazy. If I have to hear her whine one more time, I'm going to hurt her, Mace." I made my way to the lobby, avoiding the stare from the manager who was talking with some fancy, dolled-up woman with a poodle in her purse. Rolling my eyes, I walked outside, finding a private spot and noting that Finch had assigned one of my men to follow me.

"Well, you'll have to deal with her. I'm flying out to talk to Tirenti."

"But I've got the plane," I complained.

"You did. I'm stealing it from you."

"What the hell, Mason? That means I'm stuck here with her."

"You were already stuck there with her. You've got a week, and this will only take me a few days. He's hot and his son is riling him up even more. The asshole. I don't blame Donelli for wanting Angie away from him."

"At this point, I'd happily hand her over to him." The words came out oddly hollow and, as if he picked up on it, Mason stayed quiet. "Call me when you calm him down and let me know the outcome," I said to cover up.

"Will do. And Ty, don't kill her. I don't need to explain to

Donelli why my best friend murdered his daughter on their honeymoon."

"Fake honeymoon."

"Whatever, just don't kill her. And keep your hands off the staff."

"I can't make any promises." But he'd already disconnected.

With a sigh, I pocketed my phone and headed back in. The chances of surviving this were slim. Angie was like a spoiled brat who needed to be put in time-out. Everything she did grated on my nerves, but I wasn't certain what worried me more, killing her in a heated rage or fucking her in a desperate need.

My scalp was burning where Tyson had pulled my hair, but within the pain sat pleasure. The move had made me so wet that I was uncomfortable. Blowing my hair from my eyes, I leaned my head against the headboard, wondering why I was obeying his order to stay still. The idea of being stuck in this bed for days while the beach was so close irritated me. Just as much as the thought of having to share this room with Tyson. Although that thought wasn't as unappealing as it had once been. My response to him was changing, and I didn't understand why.

He'd been nothing but nasty to me...but then again, he hadn't. He'd tenderly looked at my ankle before wrapping it, then carried me into the car and the resort. And he'd staked a claim on me with his words on the plane and supported my claim on him when that wench had been hitting on him. Hearing him had made my body grow warm and left my heart thumping uncontrollably. There was a sweetness to Tyson, one he hid below his hard exterior and comments.

I looked across the room to the balcony, wondering why I cared if he was sweet and why his touch was still lingering on my skin. He'd been gone a few minutes, and I couldn't help thinking his words for the woman had been for show and he was downstairs taking her up on her offer. An odd streak of envy pinched me as my mind pictured him grabbing her hair and touching her like I wanted him to touch me.

"Damn, Anj, you're losing it. You did not just think that," I scolded myself. Needing to clear my mind, I put my feet down, peeking over my shoulder to make sure Tyson wasn't coming in. I hobbled over to the bathroom, checking myself out while I washed my hands. I was a mess. My hair looked like I'd been rolling around in the sheets with Tyson. I tried to smooth the knots out, but it didn't help. Sighing, I exited the bathroom, jumping with a scream as my eyes met his dark ones. He was standing at the end of the bed, his arms crossed, his tattoos bulging under the muscles of his forearms where he'd rolled his sleeves up.

"Do you purposely disobey me just to piss me off?"

"I don't obey anyone, so don't take it personally. And don't get any ideas, I'm not into that kind of thing."

He gave me a sly grin that sent my insides quivering. I really needed to check what that doctor had given me. Unless it was the pain making me delusional.

"I'm not getting any ideas, and trust me, I'm the furthest thing from a dom. That's more Mason's thing..." His face morphed to disgust. "Gross, that's not good. I need to have a talk with him."

"Who knew Casey was into that?" I teased, gingerly making my way to my bags and hoping his mind would stay on his sister and not on my show of independence.

"Don't put that thought in my head or I'll beat the shit out of Mason again," he grumbled, swiveling to me swiftly and grabbing my waist before slinging me over his shoulder.

"Put me down, Tyson!"

"I warned you," he said, pushing my skirt up slightly before his hand met my bare skin.

"Fuck," he muttered. "Do you wear anything but thongs?" His voice was raspy, and I couldn't deny how it sent a flurry of butterflies through my stomach.

"No, they're easy access."

"Shit, Angie. You need to stop that." He smacked my ass again, and I gave out a yelp as he threw me on the bed.

"Stop what? Dressing sexy?" I rubbed the warm spot where the sting still lingered, trying to ignore how wet those slaps had left me.

"It's not sexy, it's easy," he grumbled, standing over me.

"It's the same thing your sluts wear." I bit my tongue, knowing I'd just set myself up for a comeback.

"You're not a slut," he mumbled, surprising me. "Stop acting like you are."

He turned away and walked toward the balcony.

"Then stop acting like you are."

Glancing over his shoulder, his brow furrowing, he studied me.

"I'm no worse than you, Tyson," I said, looking away from his heavy stare and working my way down the bed.

"Damn, Anj, stop moving." He stomped back to my bags. "What do you need?"

"My hairbrush," I mumbled.

"Your hair looks fine."

I subconsciously ran my fingers through it, knowing it didn't and wondering why he was telling me it did. Opening my smaller suitcase, he started tossing things around, and I cringed. "Could you be any rougher?"

Glancing up at me, he smirked. Shit, those smirks were starting to melt me instead of irritate me like they usually did.

"I definitely can."

Rolling my eyes, I scooted closer, but his eyes shifted with an unspoken threat in them before they dropped back down. I really didn't want him going through my things and my heart pounded as I realized I didn't want him seeing any part of me that wasn't what I put on display.

"Tyson, stop," I said as he pulled my makeup bag out and turned it over in his hands, studying it.

"What is this?" he asked, unzipping the large bag and rummaging through my makeup.

"It's my makeup, asshole. What does it look like?" I snapped.

"You use all this?"

"Shut up, Tyson, and get out of my bags."

But he stood there, looking through it, picking up my concealer, then my powder, my mascara, and bunching them in his hands. He walked to the trash can and dropped them all in, emptying the entire bag as I cursed him.

"You piece of shit! Put those back." I rose from the bed, limping toward him, and he threw the empty bag into my suitcase, grabbing my wrists as I went to hit him.

"What else are you hiding, Angie? Why hide behind all that shit?"

"I hate you, Tyson."

He jerked my wrists behind me, my body pushing against his in reaction. "Well, I detest you, little viper."

"Why do you care if I wear makeup? Your whores wear it."

His face contorted, anger etched around his eyes. "I don't sleep with whores, so stop calling them that."

"Then what do you call them?"

"Women, bitch. What do you call the idiots you let fuck you every night?" The vitriol in his voice was like venom and a vein swelled in his neck. His grip on my wrists was so tight they were aching.

"Men—"

"Spoiled trust fund brats. Boys who pretend to be men."

"Shut up. At least they have class, not like the bimbos you

sleep with." I didn't know why I was so furious about the women he'd slept with suddenly. Or why it mattered to me who they were.

"Trust me, they weren't bimbos. If you'd like me to prove that, I'd be happy to call the resort manager up here and have her ride me the rest of the night."

"What do I care? This is all a sham, anyway. Go ahead and sleep with her. I don't give a shit."

His features shifted again, and I couldn't read the expression that seemed to morph from confusion to hurt to anger. It reflected the emotions that were whipping through me and when he let me go, smoothed his shirt, and walked to the door, disappointment and envy crashed through me.

"Tyson," I said, hearing the plea, the desperate need for him not to leave me alone. To not turn to another woman...even if we weren't anything more than enemies, two people who couldn't stand each other.

He paused, and I held my breath, but he didn't turn back. Instead, he left the room. Silence engulfed me, along with something I didn't like—an emptiness that sat too heavy in my chest.

I TRIED NOT to think of Tyson as time ticked by. I supposed I should have been thankful that he hadn't brought the woman back to our room. For some reason, I thought having to watch that would leave me broken in some way. I just couldn't figure out why. Digging through the trash, I returned my makeup to my bag and took it and my other toiletries into the bathroom. Evening had fallen, and I didn't expect Tyson to be back anytime soon, if at all. I was starving, having missed lunch, and now dinner was passing by, but I was too tired to ask the men guarding me for food. Deciding to get ready for bed instead, I washed my face, staring at myself in the mirror as I patted it dry. Reaching into my bag, I prepared to paint my face again, to cover the freckles and the birthmark that sat like a brown stain on the edge of my cheek.

Tyson was right. I was hiding. I'd been hiding for years, hating what I saw reflected in the mirror, the reminders of my insecurities and of the pain those freckles brought me every time I saw them. I pushed the bag aside, deciding it didn't matter tonight. I'd be sleeping here alone, so why bother covering it up? Contacts removed, I pulled my glasses out, something I never did, even at home with Tony and my father. They hadn't seen me in glasses or without makeup since I was young. No one had.

With my hands poised to release the messy ponytail I'd pulled my hair into, I stared at the version of myself that I avoided, the one I never stopped to look at before I crawled into bed each night or before I put my mask on each morning. I didn't know why Tyson's words had hit so hard or why it mattered that he'd said them. But I was tired. Tired of hiding, tired of being someone no one liked, tired of the defenses I'd built, tired of fighting with him.

After leaving the bathroom, I looked through my clothes, hating them all when I looked at them through his eyes. I glanced over at his bag. Pulling my dress off, I put a pair of shorts on, then opened his bag, avoiding the boxers and personal items and pulling out one of his T-shirts. It was dark gray, and when I brought it to my nose, it smelled like him. His smell shouldn't have been familiar to me, but it was because, as much as we hated each other, he'd been in my life for years. Long enough to recognize the way he smelled, the subtle cologne he wore.

Pulling the shirt over my head, I made my way to the stocked bar and poured myself a glass of wine. My ankle was throbbing, but I didn't want to go to bed yet. Taking my phone and my wine, I sat on the large balcony. There was a small table with two chairs, and I pulled one over to prop my leg on. I scrolled through my feed, listening to the waves crash below, the sound of music drifting through the air along with a few voices. I wondered if Tyson's was among them, if he was really with the resort manager or if he'd found another woman and was touching her.

It doesn't matter, stupid.

This was fake and in a few days or weeks, we'd go back to our lives, back to the familiar hatred that rested comfortably between us.

The sound of the door made me jump, and I braced myself, not wanting to watch him bring another woman in for me to see him with. The thought was degrading, and I knew if he did, it would completely obliterate my ability to go through with this sham. I wouldn't be able to look at him the same. I told myself it was the embarrassment of it, but I knew the truth. That deep down, I didn't want to see him with another woman because it would hurt.

"Is that my shirt?" he asked.

"So what if it is? Take your slut and find another room," I said, taking a sip of wine and not looking at him, afraid of what I'd find if I did.

He dropped a bag on the table and snatched the wine from my hand.

"Mixing—" he started, but as I looked up at him, he froze.

Shit, I hadn't expected him to come in and I was vulnerable. No makeup, no contacts, no mask. Just me. I waited for the insults, the laughter, the jabs, but none came. Instead, he lowered the wine glass and brushed his thumb over my cheek, lingering on the birthmark. I dropped my eyes, fearing his words and hating that I felt so small, so unconfident, so seen.

"Shit, Anj," he murmured. "Why do you cover that up?"

My sight leaped back to him. The hazel in his eyes was bright with a mix of green and amber, the moonlight illuminating them. There was a softness to them that I recognized from when he'd first noticed my freckles in his room. But where it had disappeared quickly then, it lingered now.

"Don't joke," I whispered.

"Who's joking? You're fucking beautiful."

My heart thudded so loud I could have sworn it was loud enough for the entire resort to hear. The air in my lungs fled with a whoosh that forced my mouth open. Words failed to form and as if he realized he'd been sweet, he turned to the bag and began taking out wrapped plates of food.

"Did you work up an appetite with that woman?" I asked, relieved that his attention had turned from me and that no woman had accompanied him into the room. "Why not just eat with her, or was she that bad at taking your cock?" The words came out with an acidity that burned my throat.

"I didn't sleep with her," he muttered, removing the cover from my plate. My mouth watered, my stomach rumbling. Fingerling potatoes, fresh green beans, and a piece of chicken that looked delicious filled the plate.

"Why not?" I asked, grabbing a green bean and chomping on it as he uncovered another plate. "Did you find someone else? One with bigger tits and lips?"

He shot me an annoyed look before he picked up my legs and sat, placing my feet in his lap.

"I didn't fuck anyone," he grumbled, rubbing his neck.

"But you could have." My voice was softer than I'd intended, and his eyes grew lighter.

"Nah, wouldn't look good if I was picking up another woman on my honeymoon, now would it?" The way he said it was sweet, and I couldn't help but smile.

He looked away quickly and stabbed some potatoes with his fork. Shoving them in his mouth, he rose and moved my feet back to the chair before walking from the balcony.

"Thank you," I said, not really knowing why I wasn't making fun of him and throwing jabs at him about not being able to get it up.

"I'd say you can thank me with that mouth of yours, but I

don't want to risk you biting me," he replied as he poured himself a glass of liquor.

"With as much of a prick as you are, I'd definitely bite," I teased, liking the way the banter between us was settling the awkwardness in the air. Even if we weren't lacing it with the usual vitriol.

"Yeah, not testing that out, little viper. You keep those teeth to yourself." He snatched my feet and sat again, taking a long drink of what looked like scotch. "Why are you wearing my shirt and why are you out of that bed?"

He leaned back, his hand still on my foot. I didn't want to tell him I liked the way his shirt smelled, or that it reminded me of him. "You said my clothes were too slutty, and I figured you'd need the bed."

He chuckled, dropping his glass to the table and tossing another potato into his mouth. "Your clothes are too revealing. You show too much skin."

"Does that make you jealous, husband?"

With a sly grin, he replied, "Would watching me fuck another woman in that bed make you jealous, wife?"

Shit, would it ever, but I wasn't about to admit that or to admit that my hatred for him was morphing into something I couldn't define. A craving was growing, one that I considered hostile because it went against everything I felt for Tyson Raines.

His hand slid up my calf, causing a flutter of nerves to tingle through my body. I needed to get control, but his words and his touch had stripped me of it.

"I..." His fingers kneaded my flesh and warmth settled in my lower belly. My breathing constricted. "No," I said, trying to reset myself, to remind myself that I hated this man. I tried to pull my leg from his hold, but he tightened his grasp on it, keeping the other secured. "I'd probably enjoy watching you fumble to make a woman come. You're such a brute. I'm sure it would give me a good laugh."

His lip twitched as if he was holding back a smile before he clenched his jaw to cover it. "You doubt my ability to make a woman come?"

I leaned forward. "Definitely."

"I should be insulted but I know what kind of men you sleep with, and I know you've never had a man who can break you the way I could, baby."

The hitch of my breath was too loud, and he released my legs, gently lowering my injured one. My eyes never left his when he stood. I sat back as he came closer, putting his hands on either side of my chair. The nearer his face came to mine, the more my body came alive.

"You don't know what a real man can do. All those boys you've been with are clumsy frat boys compared to me."

"And what are you?" I asked, resisting the urge to run my hand through his auburn curls.

"I'm a man who would ruin you for any other man."

What was happening to me? To us? I could barely breathe. My body was so turned on that I swore there was a puddle in my seat. "Would you let another man touch me once you ruined me?" I wanted to kick myself for asking, for the desperate need for him to say no that was wringing my heart.

He stepped away, the air returning to my lungs with the absence of his closeness. Taking his seat again, he eyed me, and I noticed a heaviness in the air, the anticipation that hung there along with the knowledge that his answer could change our dynamic so that we were something more than the enemies we'd always been.

"Well, little viper," he leaned forward, taking my legs in his hand, his fingers drifting over my skin so that it caused goosebumps to form while he placed my feet in his lap again, "you see, that's the thing. I don't hold on to women once I've ruined them. It's not my thing, just like you don't hold on to the men you let use you."

I pursed my lips, irritated yet relieved that he'd returned to his usual demeanor, until he said, "But if I decided to keep you..." This time the air burned in my lungs when his eyes met mine, the hazel so dark they were almost brown. "...I'd kill any man who dared lay a finger on you, I'd burn through his territory like an inferno and lay waste to anything of his until there was no trace of the bastard left to remind you of that touch."

A strange squeak slipped through my lips. All function to do anything but stare into his eyes disappeared as those words wrenched their way into my chest and carved his name into it.

He sat back again, throwing another potato into his mouth. "Now tell me why you cover those freckles up," he said, as if he hadn't just laid me to waste with his words. "And don't tell me it's because your fancy boys don't like them." He glanced over at me when I didn't answer. "Are you shitting me?"

I tugged my feet away and rose, needing to get far away from him because I didn't know how to grasp what I was experiencing or the way he seemed to turn the conversation so quickly, like he had a light switch that flicked between sexy lover to annoying ass.

"Why do you care?" I asked, intent on leaving the balcony.

He grabbed my wrist and tugged me back, causing me to land in his lap.

"What the fuck, Tyson?" I shouted, trying to pull my wrist from his hand but only moving further into his hold.

"Do you have any other words in your vocabulary besides fuck?" he asked. "With those glasses, you'd think you'd have more."

"I have lots of words like asshole, shithead, bastard, jackass," I replied, pushing at him until he released me.

"Still foul mouth words."

"Like you're any better," I huffed, limping away from him. "You use the word fuck as often as you fuck women."

"Says the bitch who can't keep her legs closed." His tone was harsh, but under it there was a sense of hurt and I wondered if I'd made the wrong move. If by pulling me back to him, he'd been giving me an opening, one I'd returned with anger and my usual bite.

"Well, they're staying closed for you, but I'm tired of being in this room. I don't care what you or the doctor says, I'm going out." I pulled a tight halter top out of my bag, ignoring his grumbles as I pulled my shirt off to change. "Maybe I'll pick up a real man who can make me come better than you and will ruin me so that I'll never need you or your stupid touch." The words had come out in haste, and I realized how they sounded too late.

I looked over at him, seeing the hunger that sat in his eyes, the fight there to not yield to it. Only then did I remember I'd started changing in front of him and my shirt was still off, revealing my pink bra with lace that was thin and see-through. There was so much tension in his muscles that his shirt was straining to rip. I wanted to turn away, to run from that look, from what it meant, from how it changed everything we were, but I didn't. Because as much as I wanted to run from it, I wanted to see where it led, to experience what Tyson Raines could do to me, even if I suspected he really would ruin me for any other man.

Chapter Seven

TYSON

Angie was killing me. After I left the room, I had every intention of taking my frustration out on another woman, but the closer I got, the further I came to going through with it. For the life of me, I couldn't explain why I hadn't. Or why a strange guilt sat in my chest at the thought.

Instead, I walked along the beach, letting my irritation simmer. She was such an annoying, stubborn-headed, foul-mouthed little bitch. One who was slowly growing on me like moss on a tree. It was something I couldn't get rid of, but something pretty and soft the closer I came to her. The more I touched her. The way her skin sat below my hands, lush and warm, inviting, and those damned freckles she hid below the layers of makeup I detested. Although I didn't know why. Most of the women I slept with wore makeup, but something about it on her bothered me.

Seeing her like that when I'd walked in with dinner had nearly destroyed me. There was a vulnerability to her when she wasn't trying, when she wasn't fighting me. And draped in my T-shirt, her cute glasses, and messy ponytail that just begged to be pulled did nothing to ease the growing attraction to her. That reaction was so unusual for me because the women I hooked up with dressed like Angie and wore thick makeup like she did. Women who were looking for the same thing I was, sex with no emotions, no attachment, just pleasure and an escape. They weren't nerdy or cute unless it was a sexy cute. Those types of women didn't hang in my circle, not with men like me. They gravitated to Mason but knew not to look my way. Well, now they didn't look at either of us because Casey would claw anyone's eyes out who dared look at Mason.

Seeing Angie like that had thrown me off guard, hitting me in a place that I sheltered, that I refused to let anyone into. And my reaction had been honest. She was beautiful that way, her brown eyes dusty with slight black flecks in them, her glasses framing her perfectly round face, the slight dimple on her left cheek showing without the mask to shadow it, and the light tan birthmark that sat just on the edge of her jawline like a mark of the gods. She'd stolen my ability to function.

Even her insults had seemed softer with her like that. I didn't know what I was thinking, rubbing her legs, then pulling her to my lap. The move had been instinctual, and I'd wanted to keep her there, to bring her lips to mine and kiss her again, but this time for real. But the moment was over and now she was blabbering about going out. Like I was going to let her walk out of the room on that sore ankle or let her anywhere near another man.

She pulled her shirt off, and I had to catch the drop of my jaw. I'd seen way too much of her skin as she'd scampered around her father's estate in her tiny bikini with the strings sitting just right on her hips, the tiny triangles keeping me from seeing her nipples which were regularly hard against the thin material that covered her perky breasts. Her body was fantastic, but she flaunted it and that annoyed me. That annoyance had grown over the years as she'd matured, and her mouth had become an unfiltered supply of insults and quips aimed at me. Ones I served up just as often.

She turned to me, a revealing halter in her hand but not as

revealing as the thin lace of her pink bra. Every inch of those perfect tits was there for me to see, and my hard-on worsened, pressing against my pants and disregarding my complaints for it to stop. Because this was Angie Donelli, not some hot woman who I could play with. This was the woman I detested who detested me just as much. But she was hot, and my body knew it.

As bad as my body's reaction to her was, her words had gripped me with a completely different intensity. She wanted another man so she wouldn't need my touch. Those words burned through me, making me desperate to keep her from another man's touch and to know how much she wanted mine. To see if she was craving it as much as I was craving hers. My jaw clenched at the thought. I didn't want Angie. I hated her, but that line between hate and lust was blurring.

She looked away from me, heading toward the bathroom. I could see she was trying to walk without limping, and it irritated me that she was still hobbling on that damned ankle when she was supposed to be resting. Rising, I snatched my T-shirt from the bed and followed her to the bathroom. She was moving slow even if she didn't want me to notice. As she closed the door, I stopped it with a hard smack of my hand. Her jump made her drop her glasses, but my eyes stayed glued to the way her tits bounced enticingly.

"Go away, Tyson," she grouched, bending down to reach for her glasses. I stopped her, scooting them out of the way and stepping into the bathroom.

"You're not going anywhere and the only bed you'll be in tonight is that one," I growled, pushing her against the wall and locking her arms over her head. I was too close to her and the position only exposed her nipples more to me. I wanted to touch them, to have them rise below the thin material. As it was, they were puckering out, tempting me to touch them, to make her moan, to make her come for me harder than she'd ever come for any other man. It was a possessive thought, and I'd never felt possessive about any woman. But the need to claim her, to own her, was there, pushing past the hatred. I had to be going mad. This wasn't a woman I wanted but being so close to her when I'd kept my distance for so many years was messing with me.

"Tyson." The breathless way she said my name tugged at me and I pressed against her, knowing how wrong this was, how it went against everything that defined us.

Her eyes searched mine, a resolve in them that was a clear acceptance of what was happening. But then, as if the same battle was happening in her, she hardened her eyes, saying, "Get off me. I'm not one of your bimbos."

"Could have fooled me," I retorted, relieved that she'd destroyed the moment, even though disappointment sat within that relief. Snapping her bra-strap, I said, "I've seen strippers show less skin than this."

Her hiss gripped me with its venom, and I saw then what I'd been blind to all those years. The back and forth we had, the aggressive battle of insults, the angst that sat between us had been a wall I'd built and one I imagined she'd built. We were too alike for her not to have. The discord between us hid the attraction, the something we could have been that neither of us wanted because it scared us both. The realization hit me like a bullet careening into my reality and shattering it.

Releasing her, I backed away, stopping whatever witty quip she was preparing to send at me by throwing my T-shirt at her. "Put this on."

"I'm going out."

"The fuck you are. You're staying here."

"To do what? Have you insult me the rest of the night or..." Her words drifted off, and I had a notion why she'd stopped. She'd been close to admitting there was something there, that thing we'd been hiding from, but like me, she didn't want it because it meant giving up too much.

"Just put it on. We can watch TV while you finish eating."

"I'm not hungry."

I glared at her, but my phone rang, pulling my attention from her.

"Yeah," I said to Mason as Angie put the shirt on.

"That's the second time you've greeted me like that, prick."

"Damn, sorry, the bitch was aggravating me."

She stuck her tongue out and tried moving past me. I was like a wall to her small frame. She wasn't petite, but she was thin and too light to move me out of the way. I bent quickly and scooped her up, throwing her over my shoulder while I talked to Mason.

"Damn you, Tyson!"

"Sounds like it's business as usual," Mason said.

"Something like that." I dropped her on the bed, ignoring her frustrated pout.

"Tirenti is up my ass about this thing with Angie. I'm heading to Armina in the morning, but that's not good enough."

That stopped me in my tracks. "Is it that bad?"

"Yeah, he's still suspicious. That asshole Joey is in his ear, saying Angie was his first. He doesn't believe you're really married. He's a scumbag, but he's smart. I'm hoping to soothe some ruffled feathers, but I'm not sure that will satisfy him. Send me pics of the two of you so I can show them the happy couple as proof."

"I'm not fucking her just for pictures," I said, ducking the pillow Angie flung at me. I had to hand it to her, she had a good arm. She was always throwing things.

"I don't care what you do with her, just send me something to show Tirenti."

Giving Angie a scolding look, I agreed to Mason's request and hung up. Angie was trying to get up again, and I shoved her back down.

"I need to get my glasses," she griped, her bottom lip protruding in an adorable pout.

"I'll get them."

I cleared the suitcases from the bed and retrieved the glasses. "Did you take your pain medicine?"

"I had my wine," she said, snatching them.

"That's not medicine."

"It is to me."

I didn't want to argue anymore. The day had been exhausting, so I let it go, grabbing the pillow from the floor and positioning it under her ankle. I wasn't sure when I'd become the nice guy, but she wasn't complaining. I imagined she was as tired of the fighting as I was.

"What are you going to do?" she asked, her eyes large and expectant. "Go to the resort bar and pick up women?"

"Nope." I found the remote and hopped into bed with her, surprised at how natural it felt. "We're stuck together." Pulling my phone out, I scooted close to her. "We're going to pretend like we're a couple in love instead of one that hates each other. Now smile for Tirenti and try not to give Joey the bird."

She let out a cute giggle, and I questioned when I started thinking her giggles were cute and not obnoxious. Dropping her head to the crook of my shoulder, she smiled into the camera. It was a beautiful smile, a natural one because she'd forgotten she didn't have makeup on. She looked up at me and I turned my head instinctually, my lips brushing over hers. The phone fell, but I left it, my hand wrapping around her neck and deepening the kiss. There was nothing but desire behind it, and she leaned into me. Her lips were soft, and she parted them, my tongue meeting hers in a sensual dance. I didn't want to stop kissing her, wanted to lose myself to the sensations that were coursing through my body and my chest.

But this wasn't right. It wasn't us, although I wasn't sure what constituted 'us' anymore because it was morphing too quickly. She pushed gently against my chest, our lips separating as our eyes met. Confusion sat in hers, the same confusion that was pounding through me.

"We should probably forget that happened," she said so softly it was hard to believe the words were what she really wanted. They weren't the ones I wanted, but I understood why she'd spoken them. The dynamic between us was a steady, consistent one. A relationship built on hatred and annoyance. The only long-term relationship I had with a woman aside from my sister and Riley, who was like another sister to me. I didn't have relationships and when a woman got close, I pushed her away, disentangling myself and turning to another.

But Angie had been in my life since Mason and I had first built an alliance with her father. She'd only been eighteen, too young for my attention to turn to her, but it had, as had the discontent between us, one that had grown into the comfortable relationship we now had seven years later. She was still young, eleven years my junior, but her age concealed her experience and the woman she'd become. One I'd continued to hate, afraid to admit there was anything other than that aggression between us.

"Yeah, that's probably a good idea," I said, not moving as my heart thudded beneath her hand.

"We can't be anything more than what we are," she murmured, a slight sadness to her voice.

"Two people who despise each other?" I asked, raising my brow.

"Exactly. I return to annoying the shit out of you and you return to throwing rude comments at me."

I loosened my hold on her, letting my fingers drift over her neck and down her arm. "Is that what you want, Anj?"

She didn't answer right away, her hand sliding down my chest, my stomach muscles tightening in response.

"I..." She stopped, her voice trembling. The trepidation that filled it was the same that was currently quaking through me. The thought that if we did this, it would change everything and neither of us knew if we wanted that change. She was scared, and I would never admit but I was terrified, hating how out of control I felt.

"I tell you what. We share this bed tonight as two people who don't hate each other." Her eyes grew wide, a mix of desire and fear within them. "We call a temporary truce, but that's all." I drew my hand from her and took hers from my chest, irritated that I liked how it felt in mine, how perfect it seemed to fit. Turning, I sat back and handed her the remote.

"That's it?" she asked, sitting back.

"That's it. We pretend that didn't happen, but we test this not insulting each other thing out for the night. Just two people enjoying a movie together."

Her eyes creased. "You're going with that?"

"What do you want me to go with?" I asked, thinking I'd read her wrong and worried that if she told me what she really wanted, I'd act on it because my body was aching to take her. I wasn't sure if that's all I wanted though and suspected that if I gave in before we both figured out what was happening that it would drive a gulf between us we'd never be able to cross. One that would spoil what we had. The thought of not hearing her throw her insults at me, of not seeing those brown eyes roll when I entered a room, of not seeing her flaunt her sexy body in front of me and covering the action up with foul-mouthed words and dirty looks, was painful.

She studied me for a moment, chewing her bottom lip before she flopped back and turned the TV on. "I want to watch a movie and pretend your tongue wasn't just flirting with mine. Pretend we're friends, not enemies who just slipped up."

"Sounds good to me," I said with a relieved sigh and putting my arms behind my head. "But none of that mushy romance shit."

"Eww, I hate those movies."

I glanced at her.

"What? That shit is nothing but lies," she said. "There's

nothing like that out there. Nothing but sex and loss. True love like that doesn't exist."

My brows furrowed as I thought about how to respond. I knew love like those movies portrayed existed. I'd seen what it had done to Riley, how it had eaten her alive until she returned to Greyson and came back to life. Had seen it in Mason and my sister, the way the two of them looked at each other. I'd known Mason since we were kids and that look was one I'd never seen. And I'd seen it in my parents. How my father looked at my mother like she was his world. How he'd grab her randomly and kiss her as if he feared losing her. How his death had destroyed her, leaving her a shell of the woman she was when she was with him.

That's why I wondered what had happened to Angie to make her think that. Or what hadn't happened. Had she never been in love? I had when I was young, but it had been a very long time since I'd let myself get that close to a woman and what I'd had then didn't come close to what I knew was possible.

"So what do you want to watch if sappy love stories are out? Porn?"

She shot me a dirty look and smacked my arm with the remote.

Shrugging, I said, "It was worth a try."

"You're gross, and if we weren't calling a truce, I'd call you a few choice words."

"Go for it. I miss your insults," I joked.

"Dirty old man."

"That's better, little viper. I'm not complete if you're not spewing nasty remarks."

Her giggle caused a tightening in my chest and the sensation disturbed me. I turned back, watching as she picked a violent action movie and settled back in the bed.

"That's what you pick?" I asked. "You live that life and you want to watch it in a movie?"

"I don't live it. I hate violence, that's Tony's thing."

"Says the woman who bashed a man's brains in with a brick." I shook my head, remembering how impressed I'd been when I'd found out she'd been the one to annihilate the guy so badly there was no part of his head left.

"He was a prick who deserved it."

"Remind me not to get on your bad side that much," I muttered.

"You won't," she answered, and I stretched my arm, sliding it behind her and pulling her into my chest. "Tyson?"

"Shush, wife. Happy couple, remember? They do things like this, so just go with it."

She relaxed, snuggling into my chest, her hand resting on my waist, and I couldn't help but think it seemed like my body had been waiting for her to fill that space. I let the thought go, intent on enjoying the peace between us for a few hours before we replaced it with the mask of indifference and spite we carried regularly.

ANGIE WAS CURLED INTO ME, our bodies tangled, my arms holding her protectively as we slept face to face. Unsure what to think about it, I laid there, observing how peaceful she was, her features soft, her mouth slightly open. She was beautiful and I could have laid there looking at her all day. Rubbing my eyes, I slowly disentangled myself from her, finally unfolding her long fingers from where they'd wrapped around my shirt. Rising, I looked down at her, seeing how she moved further into my spot as if seeking my body.

The sight sent that strange fluttering in my chest again and I cursed it, turning from her and grabbing clean clothes from my bag. I never let a woman sleep overnight. I took what I needed and sent them home or didn't bother bringing them home, taking them wherever I found them. But never did I spend the night with them, holding them or letting there be any more than sex between us.

I tried telling myself it was part of the sham, the fake marriage dictating that we act like a couple, do the normal things couples did. But my arguments weren't convincing enough. Angie was still sleeping when I emerged from the bathroom, so I left her there, nodding to Finch who was on duty outside our door and hearing him call Kimble, who emerged from the room next door just as I was passing it. Always tailing me, always on guard. There was never a time we didn't have our men with us, never a time we were truly alone. It was part of the business that took some getting used to, but death was always on the horizon, waiting to take us when we least expected.

I made my way to the coffee bar that was set up just on the edge of the beach. Angie didn't drink coffee. She didn't like the bitter taste of it, so I ordered my own and a hot tea with almond milk for her, thinking it an odd thing to know about her. Only then realizing I knew a lot about her. Over the years, her small habits, her likes and dislikes had rooted into my consciousness. I didn't know those things about her brother because I'd never paid attention during my visits, but I'd catalogued Angie's, putting to memory all the tiny minutia that made up the woman I'd so vehemently despised. It seemed an odd thing to do with someone I hated.

After a brief walk, I returned to the room, finding the bed empty, the water running in the shower. Sitting on the balcony with my coffee, I waited for Angie to emerge, wishing she'd stayed in bed so I could have crawled back in and held her longer.

Fuck, Ty. What is wrong with you?

The water in the shower turned off but Angie didn't emerge, taking her time getting ready, time standing on that ankle longer. If she kept walking on it, she'd damage it more and it would end up more than just a twist. It aggravated me how she insisted on pushing it. After what seemed forever, the door opened. By now my irritation with waiting for her had grown, my thoughts of her ankle, of not seeing her when I returned, of being angry at myself for wanting to see her were now a frustration that was brimming for release.

She walked out wearing a tiny blue bikini that barely covered her body. My jaw dropped like it did each time I saw her in one, but most times I could hide the reaction beneath my hatred for her. This time, I couldn't, and my eyes perused each inch of her, the strain in my pants growing worse the more I looked. The desire to grab her and take her hard against the wall, to rip those delicate pieces of material from her body, roared through me.

"You look like you want to devour me," she said. "I thought we were back to our animosity today."

I finally drew my eyes from her body to her face. "We are."

She'd fixed herself up, the glasses gone, her hair perfectly brushed to frame her face, the makeup back to conceal the things I loved about her. Loved? That was a strong word, one that pissed me off as much as the makeup and the tiny bikini.

"Where do you think you're going?" I asked, rising from my seat.

"To the beach. I can rest my foot while I sit in the sun. I'm not spending the entire trip locked in this room with you."

But damn, how I wanted to keep her locked in with me, to explore every part of her, to taste and touch. Running my hands through my hair, I tried to shut those thoughts up, to stop the craving that had become a hostile takeover to every other emotion I had for Angie.

"You're not leaving this room in that."

She laughed, throwing her head back and revealing her graceful neck. "You are not my father, and he lets me out of the house in this."

"I don't do the daddy kink, baby, so get back in that bathroom, wash that shit off your face, and cover your body up."

She tipped her head, her eyes dark. "Your whores don't call you daddy? With as bossy as you are, I would have thought they did."

"I don't touch whores, bitch." I'd unintentionally walked closer to her, my anger surfacing with each step. "I don't need to pay for sex."

"No, I guess you don't," she said, throwing me off because I'd expected her to give me some witty remark. "Regardless, I'm not calling you daddy. It's not my thing."

The seductive way she said it destroyed me. I grabbed her hair, twisting my fingers into it and thrusting her against me. "And what is your thing?"

We were playing a game, one that was escalating quickly because we'd unleashed something last night, something we couldn't put back.

Her breaths were coming out short and strained, each one gripping me with a force I couldn't resist. "I don't have a thing."

I gave her hair a tug, her eyes lighting. "I think you do. You've just never had the right man show you what you like."

Shit, I needed to stop because we were both playing with fire, and I wanted to burn.

"What are we doing, Tyson?" she asked, her brows furrowing.

"Shit, little viper, I think you know what we're doing."

There was a gorgeous flush to her cheeks that was fighting to show below her makeup. I wondered how wet she was, the thought killing me. Pushing her into the wall, I ran my hand down her body, the temptation to fuck her growing with every bit of warm skin I touched. I wanted her so badly that it was screaming through me, a primal need to take her, to claim her.

"You hate me," she said, a desperateness to her voice. "Passionately."

She was trying to stop this, fighting it just like I was. I searched her eyes, seeing that confusion in them again.

"I do. Despise is a better word for it."

"Then walk away, Ty. Walk away now."

But I didn't want to. As much as I hated her, that craving for her was one I could no longer fight.

"Please." The desperate plea in her voice stopped me. "Hate me, despise me, insult me, but don't do this. We can't."

She was right. We couldn't because it might fracture us and the fear that it would was enough to drown me.

"Why?" I wanted to hear her say it, to confirm that she felt the same way.

She swallowed. "Because it would shatter us, and then what would we be? I know what we are now, Tyson. But I don't know what this would do to us."

I took my hand from her hip, releasing her and rolling my neck. "Go take that fucking make-up off and I'll take you to the beach."

"I'm not taking it—"

I grabbed her by the arm and dragged her to the bathroom, letting my anger overtake the jumble of emotions that were brewing like a deadly storm in me. Shoving her to the sink, I stood as a barrier to the door, my arms crossed.

"Wash the shit off, now."

"You're a prick."

"That's better, wench. Now take it off so I can see those damned freckles." I'd slipped, trying to be an asshole and letting the reason come out.

She put her hands on the sink and looked at me in the mirror. My eyes ran the length of her body, thinking how perfectly her ass was sticking out, begging for me to take her by the hips and pound into her while I watched her fall apart in the mirror.

"Fuck," I muttered, my eyes glued to her ass. As if she read the situation, she straightened up and turned the water on.

"You could have asked nicely," she grumbled. "You don't always have to be such an aggressive shithead."

"I am an aggressive shithead. I thought you knew that." I tore my eyes from her ass, trying to calm the pressure in my pants that had me aching.

"I do. You should leave, Tyson." She was wiping her face down with a small cloth, the makeup stripped away with each swipe of her hand.

Turning my attention to her supplies that were scattered around the sink, I said, "No."

"Don't say I didn't warn you. You'd think with as hard as you are right now, you wouldn't want to see me bend over again."

I froze, peering over at her. She wore a playful, teasing smile before she turned the water on and bent over again. This time, she pushed her ass out further, leaning so close to the counter that it was protruding enticingly.

"You do that shit on purpose. Like you want my cock sinking into that." She splashed water on her face, but stopped at my words. "How wet are you, baby?"

Shit, why had I asked that and why had the thought made me even harder?

"Wet enough to soak these bottoms," she said without missing a beat before she returned to washing her face.

I didn't move, knowing I wouldn't be able to walk if I tried. When had our nasty insults turned to flirty sexual banter?

"But we're enemies," she continued, lathering up her face. "And since you hate me, these soaked bottoms will stay soaked until another man satisfies me."

She rinsed her face, then blotted it dry as my rage returned, the thought of another man reaping the benefits of what I'd sewn slashing through me like a rusty knife. I walked behind her, running my hand over her ass before pulling her flush against me. She let out a low moan as her back met the bulge in my pants. My hands moved to her hips, then over the front of her bikini, noticing the smoothness underneath. Damn, she was smooth and my dick lurched. The corner of her mouth lifted into a sly grin until I dipped my finger under the material. Her body tensed, her eyes on mine.

"No man is going to take what's mine," I growled, my other hand running up her stomach.

"But I'm not yours, Tyson. We hate each other." The raspy sound of her voice gave away her true emotions.

"You are mine. I told you, your father sold you off to me for protection. This may be a fake marriage, but make no mistake, you're mine, Angie, and I will tear down any man who touches what's mine."

Her head dropped to my shoulder, and I slipped my finger lower, sinking into her wetness and knowing I'd just pushed us to a breaking point.

"Do you want me to stop?" I asked against her ear.

"Do you want to stop?" she countered, her hand wrapping around my head, her fingers threading through my hair.

"Fuck, baby, never."

"Then don't." Her consent barreled through me like a storm I couldn't stop, and I plunged my finger into her. Her body quivered in my hands as she cried out.

I tore at her top, her breasts freeing as I swept my finger over her clit. Her nipple puckered below my hand, and I took it between my fingers, watching her in the mirror. Seeing how she fell further with each twist I made. Her stomach was shaking, her breathing so rapid it was destroying me. My eyes remained fixed on her as my finger thrust back into her. Her back arched, sending my finger further. She was dripping, and I suddenly wanted her wrapped around me. She pushed her breast further into my hand and I pinched her nipple, seeing her eyes roll back as her head pressed into my shoulder. The sight riveted me, and I could barely contain myself while I watched her clenching her legs around my hand.

Her fingers pulled at my hair, and I dropped my mouth to her neck, running my lips over it before I looked back into the mirror.

"Look at yourself, Anj. You're gorgeous coming on my fingers."

Her moan was hoarse, and she pushed down on my fingers. Our eyes locked and as I drove a second finger into her, she shattered, her climax hitting her, her body tightening around them. A series of convulsions coursed through her, and I couldn't take my eyes from how sexy she looked. Her cry was feral and, knowing I couldn't hold back any longer, I answered its call, pulling my fingers from her and jerking her hips back before freeing my hard-on.

I pushed her bikini aside and thrust into her, the sensation coursing through my body and gripping every part of me. Years of need for her, covered by hatred and anger, converged in an unrelenting need to have her fall apart for me again and to break with her as I filled her.

Yanking her hips further back, I shoved her head down to the sink, the aggression pounding through me each time she thrust her hips back to meet me. The mirror was extensive enough for me to watch, to see her face as she lifted her head, pushing against my hold on her, her eyes meeting mine. They were needy and lust-filled and I thrust harder, twisting her hair in my fingers and pulling. She moaned, a sound that pummeled through me, encouraging the storm to surge as her body quaked around me. She was so close, and I was about to come, my desire for her too intense to hold back any longer.

But I fought my release. I wanted to watch how her body moved with mine, to see the ecstasy on her face, that hunger that burned in her eyes. I pulled her hair so hard her body arched into my chest.

"Come for me again, little viper." I barely recognized my voice. She had me so turned on I was struggling not to come yet.

Her eyes blazed as I continued to thrust into her, bringing my fingers back to her clit, my other hand returning to taunt her nipple more. Her nipples were fantastic. They were so hard my mouth was salivating with the need to suck on them.

"Tyson," she cried as I moved my hand up her neck, shoving her head against my chest again. I tightened slightly, not wanting to hurt her. It was hard to hold back because I was aggressive, and I didn't think she'd ever experienced a man like me. Her body trembled and mine responded, cresting to the edge of release. Slamming her back down, I grabbed her hips, my fingers digging into her flesh, and watched her in the mirror.

"That's it, baby, come for me."

She cried out, her body gripping me so hard I could no longer contain my control over it.

"Fuck I'm gonna come," I said hoarsely. I started to pull out, intent to splatter her back since I'd been too lost in the moment to think about protection. But she pushed into me. My eyes met hers.

"Fill me, Tyson," she screamed through her climax. "I need to have you inside of me."

I'd spotted the birth control on the counter, and she'd told me she always used protection, but I hadn't come inside of a woman since I'd been a foolish teenager. The thought of it was enough to push me over the edge and I slammed into her harder, sensing her climax peak, her muscles bearing down on me and coaxing my release, which tore through me. It was so intense that it shook me to the core, my body shaking with hers, her cry mingling with my grunts until I dropped my hands from her hips and leaned on the counter.

I didn't think I'd ever come so intensely, and seeing her come with me in the mirror had only added to that intensity. Her eyes met mine as I slid from her and I realized what we'd just done, the step we'd just taken. The one uncontrollable move now changing us to something other than two people who despised each other. But I didn't know what it had changed us to or if we could ever go back because going forward was an unknown neither of us was prepared to face.

I couldn't think. My body was on fire, the flames still raking through me. I could barely hold myself up and it had nothing to do with the ankle that was numb with the rapture my body was experiencing. I'd never had a man take me the way Tyson just had, never had one own me the way he had, the way he now did. That ownership had flared through me as he sent my first climax over the cliff, sending it spiraling to a place I couldn't return from.

Having him inside of me, feeling how full he made me, how alive he made my body, had been pure ecstasy. But now, as he slipped from me, our eyes met and the reality of what we'd done hit us both. I saw it in his eyes, the flash of worry, the darkness that still sat there but had deepened.

He stepped from me, and losing his touch left me empty. I heard his zipper, and I straightened up, pulling my bikini bottom back in place and realizing we'd been so caught up in the moment that he hadn't even removed it. It had been wet before, but he'd come so hard it had seeped around him and now was leaking into my bottom. This was why I never let a man come inside of me, aside from the protective reasons. But with Tyson, I had wanted it. I had needed it. I was on the pill, and I knew from our conversation that he used protection, so I wasn't worried about it, I'd simply wanted the closeness, the experience of him emptying inside of me and knowing I'd been the one he'd lost complete control with.

I lifted my bikini top from where it had fallen in the sink. Holding it up to look at where he'd ripped it from me.

"How am I supposed to go to the beach with this, jackass?" I said, using my usual brattiness to cover the mix of emotions that were going through me. I didn't know where this left us. Our bitterness toward each other had always defined our relationship, a bitterness that had started when I'd first met him and only grown over the years, leaving no room for the attraction it had shadowed.

His eyes evaluated me, the amber shining through as they softened.

"What?" I asked, still holding the top out in front of me. I bit my lip, not sure what his look meant, suddenly self-conscious and uncomfortable with what we'd done. "We can take this back, right? Pretend it didn't happen?" I wanted him to say no, but I wasn't sure what that would do or how to handle it if he did. Hearing him say yes, though, would have hurt entirely too much.

He lifted a brow, his sexy smirk returning, and he snatched the top from my hands. "You're not going to the beach this morning," he said, his hand coming out and moving below my hair. "And we're not pretending this didn't happen." He yanked me against him, and relief settled through me. "Unless that's what you really want."

I could hear the opening he was giving me, and under it, the quiet plea for me to say no. It was the same plea that had laced my question.

"No pretending," I answered, and his mouth smashed into

mine. Desperate and hungry, the power of it made me wobble. His large hands moved to my waist, and he lifted me, sitting me on the sink.

"Get off that damned ankle," he grumbled.

"Is this where you plan to fuck me again?" I asked, as his hands reached to my bottoms and tore them off. "Hey! I liked this suit!"

"I'm sure you've got a pink one in there somewhere. Although you won't be wearing it because no other man is going to be seeing this flesh."

My heart soared at his statement of ownership. He stepped closer to me, pulling his phone from his pants.

I tilted my chin, questioning him with my eyes.

"Joey wants pictures. Let's give him a picture. He lifted his camera, but I stopped him. Reaching up and tugging at the buttons on his shirt.

"Who wears a button-down on vacation on an island?" I mumbled.

"Me. I don't do golf shirts and shorts, Anj."

Where it had once irritated me when he shortened my name as if he was a close friend, now I recognized that my irritation had been over how the sound drifted down my spine like fingers softly brushing over my soul.

I fumbled with the buttons until he dropped the phone and shoved my hands out of the way, pulling it over his head. I ran my hands up his chest, noting the strength below, the restraint in his muscles as he struggled not to ravage me. His eyes dropped, taking in my body as I traced the tattoos on his chest.

"What is this?" he asked, his fingers skirting down my stomach and dipping to follow the path of my tattoo.

"Just a little something I picked up last year."

His hazel eyes flashed with something I couldn't read as he looked up from the thin green and black viper that ran down my pelvis, its venomous head pointing toward my clit. He hadn't seen it before, his hand blocking it as his fingers had been working their magic.

"A viper?"

My breath hitched, my mind never piecing together why the reptile had been my choice. The nickname he'd so vehemently given me long ago had now become one that sent my insides flipping.

"Fuck," he muttered, backing up and running his hands through his hair.

I didn't know what to say, feeling vulnerable as I sat there naked on the sink, so my defensive attitude reacted. "It doesn't mean anything, asshole. Not everything is about you. There were plenty of other guys before you and there will be plenty after. You're not the only one who calls me viper."

My words sounded bitter, the reality of what we'd done, his reaction to my tattoo and the subconscious meaning behind it stirring my anger. I hopped down, forgetting about my ankle, and bit back the cry as pain flared through the damned thing. He caught my reaction and lifted me back onto the sink.

"Damn it, Tyson, let me down so we can forget this ever happened." I avoided looking at him, hating that he was seeing what I was only now seeing. That all this time, the animosity had covered my true emotions.

He forced my eyes back to his, inserting himself between my legs and yanking me against his pelvis with his other hand. "You said we weren't pretending," he said.

I tried looking away again, but he squeezed my chin.

"Did you mean it?" he asked.

"Mean what?"

I couldn't unsee the hurt that sat in his eyes as he said, "That I'm not the only one who calls you viper?"

"It's not a very nice nickname, you know," I mumbled, dropping my eyes.

"Answer my question, Angela."

My eyes flew to him. He had never used my full name. No one but my father ever did.

"No," I finally answered. "I'd never let anyone call me that but you, even if it isn't very nice."

His hold on my chin relaxed, his eyes lighting. "I call you that for a reason."

A flutter ran through my stomach. "You do?"

He brushed his finger over my birthmark, then threaded his hand in my hair, gently this time. "I do. The first time I saw you, you were wearing this leather jumper that was so tight I could make out every curve of your tight body. I thought it was wrong for me to be that hard for a girl who was barely legal, so I made some smart remark about cheap pleather. And you walked over to me, tossing your hair over your shoulder like you owned the place and I should bow down to you. Acting like you were thirty and not eighteen. Shit, you were so hot, and then you opened your mouth."

"I remember that," I said, leaning toward him. "You walked in like you were the shit, like everyone should fear you, and had me enthralled. You were sexy, and I hated how you smirked at me, like I was a kid—"

"You were. Shit, Anj, I was almost thirty."

"You insulted me, starting the war between us, so what? So you wouldn't touch an eighteen-year-old?"

"Exactly. I have my morals."

I threw my head back and laughed, his fingers tracing my neckline when I did. "Not many," I teased.

"Fuck you," he replied playfully. "And you were quick to dish it right back to me."

"You were an old man, a sexy old man who insulted me. I wasn't about to let you get away with that."

"Of course you weren't. So you said." He yanked me closer, and I noticed he'd grown harder while we'd been talking. "A class-climbing jackass like me wouldn't know expensive snakeskin if a viper bit him in the ass."

"That's why you called me viper all those years?"

He kissed my nose, my heart stirring at his words and the move.

"That's why, little viper."

Running my fingers along his jaw, I saw him again for the first time, my eyes open to the man I'd hated since that day, never knowing that every time he called me viper it was a term of endearment. Never knowing that he'd wanted me that first day and kept himself from acting on it out of some chivalrous morals that I'd never given him credit for.

"Where does this leave us?" I asked, unsure where we went next.

"Stuck here in this room for at least the rest of the morning."

I tilted my head, trying to figure out what he meant. He draped his fingers down my chest, causing goosebumps to rise. Skirting them over my nipple before rolling it between his thumb and his index finger, he said, "I plan to keep you busy the rest of the morning while I think about whether I want another man seeing this much skin on my wife."

My heart soared through the barriers I'd placed before it, barriers built with words of animosity for too long.

"But first," he grabbed his phone and held it behind me, "let's send Joey a little reminder that his dick isn't getting anywhere near you."

His arm encircled my waist, his hand climbing into my hair and pulling my head back before he sucked my nipple into his mouth. After a few seconds of taunting it, I heard the phone fall. His other hand squeezed my ass, pushing me into his firmness. I moaned. His teeth scraped over my nipple as I held onto him, sending my head falling back against the mirror.

"That's it, baby," he mumbled, spreading my legs further and thrusting two fingers inside of me. "Come for me again and tell me who breaks you like no other man."

His thumb hit my clit, rubbing it as he pushed his fingers deeper and I arched into him. His mouth was on my breast again and the sensations that were swarming through my body had me holding tight to his arms. I'd never had a man undo me this easily, whose very touch lit me on fire so that every inch of me was ablaze. I was so close to collapsing over the edge of oblivion that I could do no more than ride the wave. The sound of my moans echoed through the bathroom.

Tyson removed his fingers, and my body screamed for his touch. I brought my head up and met the glazed, hungry look in his eyes. I didn't want him to stop. The need for him burned through me. I snagged his pants, fumbling with his belt as he eyed me, a smirk growing on his face.

"You gonna show me why men can't keep their hands off you?"

I unzipped him and slid off the counter, but no matter that I tried not to put any pressure on my foot, I still winced.

"Damn, not now, baby. I'll continue to show you why women can't keep their hands off me."

I raised a brow, tugging his pants to bring him closer and unzipping him. "Is that going to be a problem?" I asked.

He eyed me, a gleam in the hazel. "Are you claiming owner-ship of me, little viper?"

Shit, I was, and I wanted to scream it to the world. I pushed his pants down and perused his body as he stepped from them. Damn, he was even sexier than I'd thought he'd be without clothes. Wrapping my hand around his erection, I stroked him, seeing the lust flash in his eyes.

"Damn right I am. But we can talk about that when you've thoroughly fucked me, husband."

He growled, a sound that reverberated through my body, piercing my heart and stealing it. Pushing my hands aside, he picked me up. My legs wrapped around him, and he turned, pressing me into the wall and kissing me. The kiss whipped through me like a wind funnel, raising the embers that were burning within and lighting them so that there was no control. I greedily returned the kiss as everything but his touch and the sensation of him entering me disappeared. He penetrated me hard, my breath escaping with a cry that he stole with his kiss. My world became a cacophony of sensations that left me weakened to the core. Every thrust, every groan, every touch only intensified the feeling until I tumbled over the cliffs, my climax gutting me to the core. My scream urged him on, his body meeting mine in a rhythm that had my release climbing again until in one massive surge of pleasure I broke, bringing him with me, our bodies shuddering together, his lips devouring mine in a passionate kiss that lengthened the waves that were battering against me until there was nothing else to give and I slumped into his arms.

He held me there, kissing my neck softly before walking us to the bed where he laid me down, his body encompassing mine like he never wanted to let me go. And I knew I never wanted him to, no matter how frightened that thought made me.

I STEPPED FROM THE BATHROOM, freeing my hair from the clip and hearing Tyson on the phone.

"I'll explain later," he said, his eyes landing on me. He gave me a coy grin and motioned to the bed. "Just show them to Tirenti and if Joey so much as makes a comment about her body, I'll fly over there and kill him myself."

He was on me before I could sit, snatching my towel from me.

"Hold on, Mace." There was a glint in his eyes. "I need to deal with the brat."

"I'm not a brat, asshole."

He pursed his lips before that sly grin returned. Walking to the chair, he laid the towel down, flexing the muscles in his back before he turned back to me. He was sexy in a bad boy way I'd never liked, and I absently wondered if that was because there was no other bad boy who compared to him in my mind and so I'd always steered clear of them. The muscles in his chest rippled as he walked back to me. My eyes followed the line of his tattoos, then lowered to where his pants sat low on his waist.

"Get on the bed," he mouthed as he brought the phone back to his ear.

I started to question him, but he thinned his lips, his eyes growing dark. The look stirred desire in me where there should have been none. He'd taken me so many times that morning I was exhausted. It was as if all the pent-up aggression and frustration we'd held onto for so many years as we'd ignored our cravings had come out in a storm that wouldn't stop. We couldn't get enough of each other. I couldn't get enough of him. Even now, my body seemed to lurch in anticipation as I scooted onto the bed.

"Tell me what's going on," he said into the phone. I assumed he was talking to Mason, but when he crawled over me, I suddenly didn't care.

He kissed my breast, flicking his tongue against my nipple and sending chills down my body. I'd already come more than I ever had, and my body shivered in expectation as he sucked my nipple into his mouth.

"He's a slimy little shit," he continued, as if he hadn't just made my body go weak.

His mouth traveled down my stomach and over to my hip, where he bit me gently. The move soaked me, and my legs clenched. His eyes peeked up at me, and I shot him a playful yet annoyed look, trying to determine when Tyson Raines had broken me and how he suddenly ruled my body like no other man had.

"You tell him I'll fuck her in front of him if he needs proof."

He traced my tattoo with his tongue as his finger danced over my clit. My back lurched, his next words burning through me. "But make sure he knows I'll have to kill him for looking at her body."

Mason said something back that caused Tyson to tense momentarily before his tongue sank into me. My moan was loud, and he nipped at my clit. He had done it to silence me, but it only made me cry out, and my hand grabbed at the sheets.

"Fuck off, Mace. Just keep Tirenti in check and we'll continue to play our part." He flicked his tongue over my clit to soothe it. "Isn't that right, baby?"

I was having a hard time even concentrating, let alone forming words. "Sure, jackass," I managed, trying not to sound as breathless as I was.

"And tell Joey if he even thinks about touching her again, I'll break his nose again and then every bone in his body before I gut him."

The statement of possessiveness and the lethal power behind it sent my body into a frenzy, my climax on the cusp of shattering me once again. He tossed the phone aside and wrapped his arms around my thighs, pulling me further into his face.

"Time to come for me again, little viper." His tongue slid over me before it penetrated me, his arm releasing my leg and reaching for my breast. His touch sent me over the edge, his tongue leading me spiraling to the depths as I fell apart.

When the flames finally subsided, he sat back, wiping his mouth with the back of his hand before sucking his fingers into his mouth.

"Damn, Anj, you're like a feast I'm gonna have a hard time not tasting repeatedly."

I stretched my body out, still glowing in the bliss of my orgasm. The bulge in his pants was large, and as much as I'd had him, I wanted him again. But he rose, rolling his neck as he walked to his things and grabbed a shirt. Propping myself on my elbows, I watched him, wondering why he hadn't taken me again.

"Don't worry, baby, I'll let you know when I'm ready for you take my cock again. Next time, I want those lips around me."

I licked my lips, and he gave me a devious smile.

"Sure you don't want that now?" I asked, the thought of him coming in my mouth, making me warm again.

"I didn't say I didn't want it now, but I'm gonna save that until my desperation to fuck you is so high I'll use that mouth like you've never had it used before."

The shiver that ran through me was a visible one, and he raised a brow as he rolled his sleeves up. He'd taken me harder than any other man had, making good on his promise, so I had no doubt when he wanted me to go down on him, he would use my mouth aggressively. My legs twitched at the thought, causing him to chuckle.

"Get dressed."

"Why? So I can lie around this room the rest of the day? If you're not gonna have sex with me, then it's gonna be a long day."

Shaking his head, he replied, "Trust me, I can fuck you more, but I know nobody's ever taken you as much as I just did, so I'm giving you a break until I'm ready to take you again." He had moved to the bed and crawled over me again, sliding his tongue along my body. Those embers deep in my belly burst to life again. I ran my fingers through his thick hair as he brought his mouth to mine, kissing me the way only Tyson kissed me: demanding, desperate, and delicious. My body automatically drew to his, my breasts squishing against his chest when his arm wrapped under me, pulling me closer.

Tyson wasn't a gentle lover, he was aggressive and powerful, and I loved it. But this move had a gentleness to it, his kiss softening until it shifted back to the forceful side of him I expected.

He nipped at my lip, his hazel eyes dancing in the mid-morning light that coated the room. Lifting my fingers to the corner of his eyes, I traced his jawline, the move strikingly soft like his kiss had been. It frightened me, just as I imagined the kiss had done to him, which was why he'd covered it quickly.

"What are we, Tyson?" I asked, thinking it wasn't normal for two people to fear the intimacy that came with emotions that ran as deep as ours did.

A guarded look overtook his eyes, and he tried pulling away, but I wrapped my legs around him.

"Let me up, Angie. And get dressed."

"Don't change the subject," I said. "It's not an easy one for me, either."

"Then drop it. We don't need to be anything more than this."

"But this isn't what either of us considers normal, and you know that."

His eyes searched mine, and I could see how uncomfortable I'd made him. We were too much alike to not notice, but what was happening inside of me, the way my heart had come alive, was something I couldn't ignore no matter how much I wanted to.

"Let it go, Anj. I'll take you to the beach." He gave me a quick kiss and pushed my legs from him, leaving me on the bed.

"You're an ass, Tyson," I grumbled.

"Not anything you didn't know. Now find another bathing suit, one that covers more skin, and let's go."

He walked out onto the balcony, scrolling on his phone. With a sigh, I rose from the bed, hobbling on my foot and cursing my ankle like I wanted to curse him.

"So, what now?" I asked as I pulled out my pink bikini, not caring that he wanted me covered up more. "We just go back to being enemies until you're ready to fuck me again?"

He remained quiet, and I kept my back to him as I stepped into my bottoms. I was sure I'd pissed him off, but I didn't care. I was good at pissing him off.

I felt his fingers on my neck before he turned me and thrust me into his body. His eyes were shadowed, his jaw clenched, the grip on my neck soaking me along with that steely gaze.

"What are you going to do, Tyson? Call me names, insult me to cover up what this is? If so, then let's do that because I'm scared of what this is...as scared as you are, and I'm comfortable with your insults and your hatred." My heart was pounding so loud it was thudding in my ears.

"You're a bitch, Angie."

"I'm a bitch you've now touched and can't run from like you always do." His eyes narrowed, his jaw clenching more. "Just like I can't run from you like I always do."

He relaxed his grip on my neck and his fingers weaved through my hair.

"Neither of us knows how to do this, Tyson. And that's okay."

He pushed my face closer, kissing me as if the world was ending and this was our last kiss. It left me breathless, and when he released me, I teetered.

"That's not what you're planning to wear, is it?" he asked, as if he hadn't just melted me into a useless puddle. "You look like a tramp."

So that's where we were going. Returning to what we'd been, the comfortable ease of nasty banter that let us avoid the situation, the feelings, the revelations we'd had.

"Too bad. Maybe I can pick up some real men while I'm out there," I retorted playfully. "I hear they know how to make me come better than the boys I usually have sex with."

His jaw clenched more, but his eyes sparkled with humor. Giving my ass a smack, he walked away, pouring himself a glass of liquor. When I finished dressing, I pulled a pair of heeled sandals from my bag.

"What the hell are those?"

"What do they look like, asshole?"

"No." He took them from my hand and tossed them across the room.

"How am I supposed to walk to the beach?" My frustration with him was returning, and it felt good.

"You can barely walk in bare feet. Wearing those things will break that goddamn ankle."

I put my hand on my hips, pouting my lip.

"Keep that lip out like that and I'll put it to use."

"Fuck you, Raines."

"I already had a piece of that, baby. Save it for later."

I grumbled as I walked toward the bathroom. "I'll save it for some hot guy on the beach."

He had his hand locked on my arm before I could make it any further. Twisting me around, he picked me up and flung me over his shoulder.

"Put me down, Tyson!" I hit his back, but he only laughed, sliding the material of my suit over and rubbing my ass before he smacked it.

"Ouch!"

"Damn, I like that ass," he said, leaving the room.

"I need to finish getting ready," I complained.

Tyson's man followed us down the hall, talking into an earpiece.

"I believe I told you no more makeup."

"But—"

"No buts. That shit's going in the trash when I get back." He gave my ass another smack and his man tried to hide his smile. I shot him a dirty look, but his grin only grew. By now, a second man had joined him, both of them getting a good laugh out of my position.

"Damn it, Tyson, my suit is coming off." The tie had loosened precariously, and I knew when he put me down, I'd be flashing anyone in sight.

"You'd better make sure you have those tits covered when I put you in that sand or I'll be burying anyone who sees them."

With a sigh, I decided it wasn't worth complaining anymore.

Besides, his last comment held a sweetness to it I was sure only I picked up on. I clung to his back, ignoring the stares of the people in the lobby and shooting dagger eyes at the resort manager as we passed her. Tyson was mine now and if the bitch so much as looked at him, I'd scratch her eyes out.

The thought was a foreign one, and I wasn't sure when this possessive need to have Tyson to myself had surfaced, but now that it was there, I wasn't letting it go. Just like I wasn't letting him go, no matter how that idea challenged everything I was.

Chapter Nine

TYSON

Angie Donelli. The woman I'd despised for years was now a woman I'd kill for. As hard as I'd fought my need for her, she'd broken me. I'd taken her repeatedly, unable to stop touching her as if I was making up for all the years that I hadn't. Even now I wanted to pick her back up and slam her against the side of the resort and hear her cries. To have her body crumble with mine.

I squeezed the glass, trying to calm my thoughts as I waited for the bartender to fix Angie's drink. A damned girly drink and, of course, it was a pink. Just like her damned bikini, the one that showed almost all of that sexy body to anyone who was looking. And they were looking.

"Boss," Finch said, moving next to me. "We've got a problem."

I picked my eyes up from the bar, my brow cinching. "What kind of problem?"

"The male kind. Your wife seems to have attracted some attention."

I'd left her for ten minutes and she couldn't keep herself contained. The thought of her flirting with another man sent a venomous sting of jealousy into my system. She was likely doing it to get back at me for not answering her question. What were we now? It was a question I couldn't answer because I wasn't ever a 'we'. There was never a time when a woman was more than satisfaction, a means for release, for escape. But Angie was different, and she knew it, just like I did. I just wasn't certain if I was ready for that difference, and I suspected from her reaction that it was the same for her. Both of us had kept sex separated from anything that could hurt us. And now we'd crossed that divide. I know I had.

I glanced back at the beach. She was still under the umbrella where I'd placed her, her luscious body spread out on the blanket, her blonde hair dark in the umbrella's shade. She had her knee at an angle, and I remembered how soft the skin had been as I'd touched and licked it. Even the thought of it made me hard.

"Shit," I muttered, adjusting myself and throwing some cash to the bartender, who had finished her drink. I motioned for Finch to take hers and I grabbed my scotch, casually walking back to where two college age boys were standing over her. Their eyes were all over her and I gritted my teeth, wishing I could pull my gun out and shoot them both.

That move would land me in prison with this many witnesses, and I preferred to keep my illegal acts under the radar of the cops.

"I don't remember giving you permission to talk to strangers, baby," I said, staking my claim as I came up to them. "Is there a reason you boys are ogling my wife's body? Because I can assure you it's taken and anyone who tries to touch it will lose a few fingers...if I'm in a good mood."

I stared them down, seeing how they swallowed uncomfortably. The one backed up, but the other didn't move.

"Do you know who I am?" he asked.

I looked him up and down. "I don't think you know who *I* am."

"Do I give a fuck?" he asked, causing me to chuckle.

I sat my drink down, rolling my sleeves higher and seeing him eye my tattoos. I may have dressed the part of a classy man, but take off the expensive button-downs and dress slacks and I was a lethal machine who would butcher anyone who messed with me. I spent my days pounding my fists into punching bags and my nights pounding them into dirtbags. And my body reaped the benefit. I was built, and the way his eyes shifted from side to side as he tried to come up with more bravado was entertaining.

"I think you do, Charlie. Charles Von Kenting the third, son of the governor of *my* province." I emphasized the word my so he understood who really ruled our province. "Second son, I might add. Your older brother is in line to take your father's position and you...you spend your time squandering his money in establishments like mine, on women and gambling, thinking you're some big player."

He took another step forward, and I saw Finch reach for his gun. Giving him a hand signal, I told him to stand down. This kid didn't worry me. Neither did his father, who remained in power only because Mason and I had taken down a threat to it. We owned the province, not the governor.

"Why don't you go ask your daddy who I am?" I glanced behind him, seeing that his father had caught sight of the interaction, a worried look on his face. I gave him a nod, which he returned with a relieved wave back at me. "And keep your eyes off my wife or I'll ensure you never look at another woman again."

I turned my back on him and his buddy, not caring that his eyes were burning holes into my back. He would run off and tell his father, who would educate him not to mess with me. Drink in hand, I took a gulp and eyed Angie, who was looking up at me. Her brown eyes were ripe with excitement, and I gave her a naughty smile.

Finch handed her drink to her and moved to the side so he could keep watch.

"I turn my back for five minutes and you're already making trouble?" I asked, sitting next to her.

"I wasn't causing trouble," she said, not looking at me. "And do you have to be so mean?"

"Mean?" I asked. "I thought I went gentle on the kid. He still has his body parts intact."

She turned to me. "Gentle? You humiliated him in front of his friend and me."

I gritted my teeth. "You? Why do you care if he's humiliated? Did I interrupt something?"

The roll of her eyes was her attempt to annoy me, but it was too cute. "I'm not yours, remember? We're going back to what we were before this morning, which means I can flirt all I want."

She was being a brat and, as fired up as I already was, the move was a dangerous one.

"Isn't that what we agreed?" she continued.

"Don't be a stupid bitch, Angie."

"I'm not stupid," she grumbled.

Laughing, I said, "But you are a bitch."

She smacked me and I yanked her over so that her body was on mine. The move excited my dick, which caused my pants to tent in anticipation. "Don't tempt me to smack that ass again."

"You wouldn't dare. Not here," she said, her eyes going wide.

"No? I don't give a shit what any of these people think. I'll pull your bottoms down and spank you while they all watch. Then I'll keep them off and fuck you right in front of them."

She tried to pull from me, but I overpowered her, flipping her onto her stomach. "Damn it, Tyson," she complained as I yanked the edge of her bottoms up and laid a loud smack on that beautiful ass.

She yelped until I smoothed my hand over the sting, her yelp changing to a moan that had me yearning for more.

"Do I need to show those boys how a real man makes a

woman come?" I asked, leaning close to her ear and sliding my hand between her legs.

"No," she said, a distinct rasp in her voice.

I was tempted to. To have her come undone while my fingers were deep inside of her, but I didn't want anyone else seeing how sexy she was when she did. I wanted that for myself, and I wasn't about to share it. I lifted from her body, cursing myself for becoming so lost in her that I had become possessive, thinking of her as mine. When had that need taken hold of me?

"You're a bastard," she said, sitting up and rubbing her ass. Her cheeks were flush, the freckles highlighted within the rosy color. Unable to resist, I reached over and ran my finger over them. She was too beautiful, and I'd always known it. That's why I'd always hated that she covered her beauty up with makeup as if she didn't see it. I'd known from the first time I saw her, there was natural beauty underneath. I just never realized how right I was or what the sight of it would do to me.

Her eyes were light chestnut as they studied me, trying to determine why I'd turned gentle. I didn't want to hurt her. I'd never do anything to her that caused her genuine pain, but I was aggressive and I enjoyed taking women that way. And something about her heightened that aggression. I supposed it was the unfriendly banter we'd had for years that would always be an undercurrent to whatever this was. But I'd never hurt her in any way that didn't cause her pleasure.

"Tyson," she said, bringing me from my thoughts. "Aren't you going to say something nasty to me?"

Giving her a smile, I said, "I'm trying to think of something that won't make me want to rip that bikini off and devour you."

"Spanking me gets you that hot? I thought you didn't have that daddy dom kink." She was being playful, and it only encouraged me to want her more.

"Nope, not me, baby. I'm an aggressive alpha. I'm not into that spanking thing, but spanking your ass gets me so hard I can't help it. Maybe it's something about that bratty attitude of yours that I need to spank out of you."

"I'm not calling you daddy," she said, laying back on the blanket. "And can you take this damn umbrella off me? How am I supposed to enjoy the sun with this thing blocking me?"

"I'm not sitting in the sun. Sitting here is irritating enough."

"Then go back to the room and do whatever it is you do. I want to stay out here."

"You're annoying, Anj." I didn't want to leave her out here alone, but I hated sitting around. I needed to move and with as much confusion as the last few hours and even the last day was giving me, a few hours in the gym would do me good.

"Well, go be annoyed someplace else."

I moved over her again, grabbing her face and turning it to me.

"Are you going to pout?" she asked with a nasty sting to her voice. That familiar tone always sent my blood boiling.

"You're going to be pouting when I put those lips to use later." I kissed her, enjoying how her body went limp below mine. Kissing her woke a part of me that had always been dormant. It was one I didn't want woken because I didn't want attachment. And her kisses reached in and anchored me to her. I drew back, seeing the emotion in her eyes and not liking it because it was the same that was pounding through me like a hostile enemy trying to take over me.

"Be a good girl and no flirting, or I'll have to get violent and that'll piss Mason off."

"I can't promise anything," she said as I rose, brushing the sand from my clothes. "It might be fun to watch Mason and you in a fight. Two sexy men, all those muscles and tattoos."

My brows creased as I glared at her. "Don't even try flirting with Mason. My sister will kick your ass and then I'll spank it."

"Not going there again. Casey scares me and I wouldn't dare touch her man. But that doesn't mean I can't touch her brother."

She gave me a sexy wink, then complained to Finch about moving the umbrella.

He looked at me, and I shrugged. "I'd listen to her, Finch. That mouth of hers won't stop until you do and trust me, it's annoying as hell unless it's busy."

And damn, did I want to keep it busy. Shaking my head, I left her, knowing Finch would keep her safe. I heard him call for backup as I walked away, Creek trailing behind me.

I SPENT the next two hours in the gym, taking my frustrations out and trying to work through the emotions that were building uncomfortably in me. It didn't help, and when Creek walked in, telling me the governor from our province was outside waiting to talk to me, my mood only soured more. He was a frequent guest at the resort. Sometimes he brought his family, sometimes his mistress of the month. We didn't care; it gave us more power over him and having him think he had the control when he didn't was part of the fun.

"Send him in," I said, grabbing a towel and wiping my face.

Charles Von Kenting the second walked in a few seconds later, looking as proud and stuffy as he usually did for a man who was a notorious cheater both on his wife and the province. His hands were so dirty it made me and Mason look like angels. Only we knew everything he did and encouraged it, his frequent visits to the club, the private rooms, the women, the gambling. His younger son was following in his footsteps, which only helped us keep Chuck senior in line.

"Tyson," he said with a quick nod.

"Chuck. And what reason would you have to leave your lovely wife's side during your annual family vacation?"

He cleared his throat, looking around to make sure we were alone.

"I don't allow anyone in my gym when I'm in it," I said to reassure him.

He wiped his hands down his designer shorts. "I wanted to thank you for letting Charlie off earlier. I hope he didn't do anything to upset you."

I looked him up and down before walking away to toss my towel in the laundry bin.

"Your son hit on my wife, then challenged me. Not the smartest kid."

The perspiration glimmered on his forehead. "Your wife? I hadn't heard—"

"I don't make my personal business anyone else's, Chuck." I made a point to lift my shirt to wipe my face, noting the widening of his eyes. He wasn't a small man and for a man in his fifties, he looked good and fit, but he wasn't me. "It was a quick marriage, small ceremony."

"Oh, congratulations?" I hardened my gaze at him, not liking the implication with the inflection of the word as if I'd knocked Angie up.

"Are you implying that my wife had to force my hand, Chuck?" I said, moving closer to him.

"No, of course not," he said hastily.

"Good, because no one forces my hand, and it would insult my wife to hear that's what you assumed." And damn would it. I could hear her now, going off on him with those dirty words and untethered remarks. She was a spitfire, and I had to clear the thought from my head before my sweats tented.

"Make sure your son keeps his mouth shut and respects the women in this resort. He may think he's the shit, but I can guarantee there are plenty of people here who are worth more and who hold more power than you." I pulled the collar of his shirt, giving it a good tug as I straightened it.

"Certainly, Tyson. I apologize for anything he did and take full responsibility for it."

"Good. Remember Chuck, Mason and I put you in that office by making your opponent disappear. We can remove you from it just as easily."

His eyes darted nervously, his tongue flicking out to lick his lips in reaction. "Understood."

"Go spoil your wife like you do your mistresses, Chuck. Dinner is on me tonight."

"Thank you, I'll do that." He backed away, bumping into Creek, whose steely eyes would have made most men run in fear. To his credit, Chuck kept his steps steady.

"Oh, and Chuck." He stopped, his hand on the door handle. "If your son so much as looks at my wife again, I'll cut his dick off and give it to her as a honeymoon gift."

I saw the shake of his hand as he pulled the door open, muttering a "Yes, sir," as he left.

Rolling my neck, I caught Creek's eye. "Really?" he said.

"Are you questioning my methods?"

"No, boss. Just thinking of Angie's reaction if that's what you brought her in a gift box."

My laugh was loud, the image making it hard to catch my breath. "Shit, that mouth wouldn't stop cussing me out. I wouldn't hear the end of it. Speaking of mouths," I said, looking at my watch.

"She's back in the room," he said, reading my thoughts and giving me a crooked grin.

"Good, because I have plans for that mouth that don't involve any cussing but my own." The thought was enough to make me uncomfortably hard.

He shook his head as we left the gym.

I made my way back to the room, stopping on my way up to ensure the governor and his family enjoyed their meal on me before I headed upstairs. Angie was on the balcony, the sun high-lighting the golden strands in her hair. She had her leg propped, and I followed the path up to where her sundress sat near the top of her thigh. She turned, her brown eyes lit to a light hue, her smile reaching them. The dress tied around her neck, dipping in a sexy v so the flesh of her breasts was prominent. She was hot and I couldn't stop my body's reaction to her.

"I ordered us dinner," she said, and I dragged my eyes from her body to the table to see that she had indeed ordered dinner, a bottle of red wine in the center. "I hope you like steak."

"One of my favorites. I like it rare, juicy, and flavorful."

Her cheeks grew a delicate shade of pink, and I skimmed my fingers over one.

"I think you owe me something first," I said, dropping my fingers to her lips.

She arched her brow. "Do I?"

"Oh yeah. I told you, those lips needed to be around my cock tonight, baby."

She looked me over, frowning. "Weren't you just at the gym? For a few hours?"

"Yeah, and I'm ready for some pleasure now."

"Uh, no." She turned back to the table.

"Excuse me?" My jaw ticked.

"You just worked out. Go take a shower."

"All those guys you pick up in clubs, who've had their junk in other girls and their balls sweating on dance floors, and you want me to take a shower?"

She gave me a look of disgust, her nose turning up. "I'm never someone's sloppy seconds. And I'm not putting my mouth anywhere near you until you've showered." She picked up her glass of wine and took a deliberately slow sip.

"You're such a brat," I complained, but she didn't look back at me. I wanted to yank her from the seat and force her to her knees, but she was the kind of girl who would bite without remorse. "Fine. Damn obnoxious spoiled little cunt," I mumbled, stomping away.

"Those insults won't help your case, shithead."

I stopped in my tracks and glanced over at her. "Get your ass up from that chair and in that bathroom."

"I don't take orders. I'm not your sub, Tyson."

My fists were clenching so tight by now I was about to punch a hole in the wall. "Angela, get out of that chair and into the bathroom. If I have to shower, so do you."

"I just showered," she complained.

I turned the water on and waited for her, knowing she'd come because she was too annoying not to. I tried to ignore the limp she was trying to hide from me and the guilt that gnawed at me for forgetting to keep her off her feet.

"I didn't think you needed a babysitter," she snapped as I pulled my shirt over my head, the guilt fading as my anger rose again.

"Shut up, Anj and get in the damn shower."

I tossed my sweats and boxers off, sensing her eyes on me when I stepped under the water. Running it into my hair, I peered over at her. Irritation lit her eyes, but it was coated with a dusting of desire that had my balls tightening.

"Don't expect this command thing to be a normal thing." She reached back to untie her dress as she drew closer to the shower.

"I don't. Leave the dress on."

Her eyes bulged, her lips pouting out.

"That's exactly how I want those lips, baby."

"Are you kidding me? This dress is silk, the water will ruin it, and it's one of my favorites."

I moved from the water and grabbed her neck, pulling her mouth to mine and kissing her. She resisted for a second before her mouth was as greedy as mine, and I yanked her under the water.

"Damn you, Tyson," she muttered against my lips. "You ruined my dress."

"I'll buy you ten more like it so I can ruin those, too. Now get on your knees and remind me why that mouth turns me on so much."

"I thought it was my insults," she purred.

"Something like that." Water soaked her hair, dripping down the edge of her nose. She looked adorable, but as she dropped to her knees, her tits bouncing as her nipples pushed through the soaked material, she looked sexy as hell.

She licked her lips, her delicate hands grasping my shaft. Looking up at me with those big chocolate eyes, she ran her tongue along my tip in a seductive circle. The sensation left me weak and when she took me into her mouth, I put my hand out against the shower wall to steady myself.

"Fuck, little viper," I growled as her tongue slid over the bottom of my shaft before she dropped so deep, I hit the back of her throat. Her gag was slight, but enough to throw the storm in me into a violent surge that swept through my entire body. Threading my fingers through her wet hair, I grasped the strands and shoved her further. Her body shuddered, her eyes closing, the moan she elicited buzzing over my shaft. "Eyes on me, baby. I want to watch what taking my cock does to you," I said, thrusting into her, then pulling her back to give her air.

She breathed deep, her eyes on me, large and watery. "Are you going to call me your good girl when I swallow?" she cooed rather breathlessly.

"Shit, no. You're far from a good girl. I don't fuck good girls, and they don't take my cock as deep as your naughty mouth does. Now shut up and go back to using that mouth the way I told you to."

She shivered, and I shoved her back on me. Her mouth easily accepted me even with as large as I was. I tried not to think of all the men she'd gone down on to be this good because I'd had my fair share of blowjobs, enough for me to know what I liked. But the thought still spurred the fire in me, and I steadied her head, owning her mouth like it was the last thing that would ever be around me again. Her manicured nails dug into my thighs, and I yanked her from me, knowing I was close to coming and her gags were about to drive me over the edge.

The line of spit that followed quickly washed away leaving only water droplets that hung like sexy beads from her bottom lip. She reached up and pushed my hand away, giving me a determined look before she grasped my dick and dropped over it, her head moving in rhythmic bobs that drove me crazy. I threw my other hand out and held on as she took control, taking me so deep and hard that it sent me over the edge. My fingers dug into the tiled wall, and my pelvis thrust as I dropped my hand and shoved her into me with each rush of release that gripped me until there was nothing left.

Letting her head go, I tried to catch my breath. Her eyes were on me, a glint of amusement in them while she swallowed in an exaggerated fashion. The water was splashing over her as her tongue swept out and she brought her finger to her lips, wiping the corner of her mouth seductively before she opened her mouth to show me she'd swallowed it all. Shit, she was something. She tipped her mouth up and held her tongue out to let the shower water fill her mouth, then swallowed it.

The move had me growing hard again, and I knew as drained as she'd left me, I wanted more of her. I grabbed her by the neck and brought her up, slamming her against the wall and tearing her dress from her. My hand scooped her leg up to protect her ankle while I sucked her nipple into my mouth. With the moan that came from her and the sensation of her fingers sinking into my hair, I could barely think. My need for her was so intense that I didn't know if I could ever stop touching her. I hated how easily she broke me, how desperately I wanted her, how much deeper I was falling with every touch, every look, every taste of her. And as I took her again, I didn't want to imagine not hearing my name fall from her lips as she came undone for me every night for the rest of my life.

Chapter Ten

ANGIE

Tyson's hold on me was powerful. His hand had mine pinned against the tile, his other hand was holding my leg against his thigh in a grip so tight I was quivering. There was an intensity to him that was two-fold what it normally was, like something had cracked in him when I'd gone down on him. Watching him come as I'd had him in my mouth had been one of the sexiest things I'd ever seen. Everything about Tyson was sexy and having that control over him had heightened the experience. I'd loved every second, even the aggressive face fucking he'd given me. I was so wet I'd almost come with him.

Now, as he devoured my breast, his hands holding me, I was so close to losing it I didn't think I could take much more before he destroyed me completely. I tightened my leg around him, ignoring the flare of pain in my ankle as my heel dug into his ass. He loosened his hold on my thigh, his hand caressing my ass before his fingers slid into me. I jerked against him, and he chuckled against my breast. His fingers wrapped around the fingers of my other hand as he held it pinned to the wall, and I absently wondered at how perfectly my hand fit in his.

The fire in me flared looking for the release his fingers

promised when they rubbed my clit. I cried out, my body shaking as the climax built in me, but he smothered my cry with his mouth, his kiss greedy and demanding. A demand I answered until his mouth dropped against my neck, the warmth of his tongue sending goosebumps pebbling over my skin.

"Fuck, baby," he muttered, that nickname doing what it always did to me, melting me with the ownership it now held, the claim that was inherent in it. "You're killing me." His voice was muffled, but I heard the desperation in it, the admittance that whatever this was between us had crossed so far past the line that he couldn't deny it any more than I could. Yet we both would, because that's who we were.

His fingers left me, and I couldn't stop my disappointed cry. But he only laughed, lowering his body, his tongue tracing my skin until he was on his knees. My body shook in anticipation because his tongue was amazing and the climax it had evoked from me earlier in the day had been better than any I'd had. Lifting my leg, he tossed it over his shoulder and grasped my ass, pulling me into his face. I moaned his name, feeling his smile against me as his tongue plunged into me.

Closing my eyes, I arched my back, letting my head fall against the tile and his tongue sweep me away. Every nerve in my body was awake, pleasure coursing through me and leaving me weakened. I pushed at his head the closer I grew, the impending release cresting inside of me, blocking out the sound of the shower, the sensation of the water pelting my skin, the sting of my ankle. Nothing existed but the pleasure Tyson was bringing me and as my body came undone, falling apart like the shattering of glass, I screamed his name. It was a feral cry that came from an untapped part of me. My body trembled, my leg giving out, and I fell into his arms as he rose, catching me and shifting my legs around him, penetrating me with a powerful thrust that reawakened me. I clasped to his shoulders and his lips crashed into mine, his tongue searching mine out as if not reaching it would tear him apart.

All thought, all reality, everything faded and only Tyson was there, our bodies becoming one as he took me so hard another climax tore from me, his mouth stealing my cry. I didn't know how to do anything but ride the tide of ecstasy that was burning through me and as another orgasm built, ascending with his before ripping through me like an untethered storm I didn't know how I could ever belong to another man because Tyson owned me like no other had. The thought was enough to destroy me but the feel of him filling me, his body shaking so intensely with his release that he had my body pinned between him and the wall left me barely able to breathe while the remains of my climax shivered through me.

He pinned my hand over my head again, weaving his fingers into mine and when he drew back, his hazel eyes were shadowed. I knew then that he was struggling, just as I was. That we'd fallen past a point where we could continue as we had, but neither of us knew how to get back to where we'd been and moving forward was terrifying for two people like us.

TYSON HAD CARRIED me into the room and placed me in the bed, our bodies gravitating toward each other again until we were both so worked up that we'd had sex again. It was hard and dirty because that's what we both knew. Making love was what it would have been if we were two people who didn't shield our emotions and hide from that term. But as we lay there, my head on his chest, his fingers gliding through my hair, I thought maybe that's where we were heading...if we weren't already there.

I peeked up at him, seeing how content and relaxed he was, my heart leaping at the sight, then pounding hard as he looked back at me.

"You ready to go again, little viper?" he asked.

With a laugh, I looked down, tracing a random tattoo on his chest and staring at the shape within it. "No, I haven't been this worn out in years. I think you may have broken me." The moment the words left my mouth, I realized what I'd said, the power of the underlining meaning of them. His chest went still, his fingers stopping their gentle caress of my hair.

"Is that all it takes to break you?" he asked, but I heard the emotion beneath the tone.

"Almost," I answered, looking closer at the tattoo. He grabbed my hand as recognition settled in.

"Don't," he said, his tone harsh.

"Tyson—"

"Angie, don't go there." It was a plea I couldn't ignore as I stared at the small black viper that was laced around the dagger. "It means nothing."

I glanced up at him, seeing the fear that lay behind his hard eyes. And I knew it meant everything, just like my tattoo did. Small subconscious ties to each other, a piece of him to carry with me, a piece of me to carry with him. We couldn't find a way to peel back the layers of hatred we'd built to cover our true feelings, but they found their way through. I dropped my eyes and jerked my wrist free.

"Don't be an asshole, Tyson."

"I am an asshole, Anj. Now get the hell off me and go to sleep."

I picked my head up and glared at him. "Not this time, asshole."

Fury burned behind his eyes, only increasing when I straddled him. "What are you doing, Angie?"

Hands leaning on his chest, I looked into his eyes. They shimmered with a blend of annoyance and humor, but I couldn't tell which one was stronger.

"Are you trying to take control of me?" he asked, his smirk forming and threatening to send my insides into turmoil.

"Maybe," I purred.

He brought his finger up and followed the path of my freckles, emotion in his eyes that he shadowed when he caught me watching him.

"Why do you hide them?" he asked.

He was avoiding talking about the tattoo, which irked me, but with a sigh, I gave up pushing him, knowing it would only piss him off again. And as much as I enjoyed him like that, I was enjoying this moment more.

He continued to caress my cheek, so I leaned into it, saying, "They remind me of my mother."

His eyes flashed to mine, creasing as he tried to understand. It was something I'd never shared, keeping it to myself where I kept all my emotions aside from disgust or annoyance.

"My mother was beautiful. She could walk into a room and command everyone's attention with just her presence. I was young when she passed, but I remember how I'd watch her, so graceful and confident. She was classy, never flaunting her body, but knowing how to dress her curves. Her beauty was natural and enchanting—sun-kissed skin, hair that I loved tangling my small fingers in, and the largest brown eyes that when they fell on you lit you from the inside out."

I stopped, pushing back the surge of sadness that wanted to sneak past my borders. Tyson waited, his eyes intently watching me while his fingers played in my hair. Taking a breath, I continued. "She would tuck me in each night, and kiss each one of my freckles, ending with my birthmark and telling me how it was special. A sign that the gods watched over me, she would say. And no matter how the other kids made fun of me for it, her words emboldened me." The memory of the teasing was one I'd squashed along with the memory of her words, and remembering them hurt. "My father called us twins we looked so much alike, and I loved that, because my mother was the standard of beauty for me...until she died." I dropped my eyes, noticing how my thumb had been subconsciously tracing his viper tattoo. "I was only ten when she died, but every time I looked in the mirror, I saw my mother. As I aged, I could see it in my father's eyes, the sadness there when he looked at me. I covered the birthmark first when the teasing overshadowed the memory of her words."

Tyson's thumb brushed across it, and I looked back up at him. "And then the freckles. Each time I covered more, my father relaxed when I entered a room. My brother's eyes no longer seemed so sad. The clothes came next, as I cleaned out everything that reflected what she'd taught me about fashion, replacing it with more skin, less material. And by the time I was sixteen, my glasses were gone, and my hair was lightened. There was nothing left to remind me of her, nothing left but the emptiness in my chest, which I filled with my pettiness, my demands, and my attitude. All things that went against everything she was."

I looked back down, the guilt I'd hidden away with everything else surfacing. He tipped my chin up, forcing my eyes to his.

"So you're telling me you're not a natural blonde?" His question brought only relief that he didn't judge me for dishonoring my mother's memory, for burying my emotions, and for being the brat he'd always known me to be.

"Guess you had no way of knowing," I replied playfully.

His other hand rubbed down my smooth body. "That's just downright deceitful. What color is your hair, baby?"

Unable to stop my smile, I said, "Strawberry blonde."

"You're a red-head and you hide it? Shit, that's even hotter. You're growing that out. No more dye jobs for you." He yanked me off him and flipped me, hovering over me in a protective position. "No more hiding from me," he said.

"But Tyson..." I didn't want to say it, to ruin the moment with the truth.

He wrapped his hand around my waist and pulled me against him, my back rising from the mattress. "What, Anj?"

"You can't expect me to make those changes when we...we..."

"When we what? Hate each other?"

"Yes."

"Of course I can because I own your bratty little ass, no matter how much you annoy the shit out of me."

My smile threatened to escape. "You don't own me. It's temporary until this shit with Joey calms down. Then you have to give me up." Saying it burned my throat, and I saw the flinch he tried to hide from me.

"We'll deal with that when the time comes." He rolled from me and rose, walking across the room and grabbing his phone. I propped myself on my elbows, watching his ass and loving how the muscles in it and his thighs moved.

"Stop licking your lips like that, Anj, or I'll put them to use again."

He brought the phone up to his ear, and I wondered what he was doing until he turned and I took in the sight of him from the other angle again. There was no stopping how wet it made me and, as if he knew, he threw me a lopsided grin.

"Get us some dinner," he said into the phone. "I don't care if you already brought her dinner. It's cold."

There was a moment of silence, one I took to peruse his body again.

"Whatever you brought last time is fine."

He hung up, and walked to the bar, pouring himself a glass of liquor before walking to the balcony and grabbing the bottle of wine and my glass. He didn't seem to care that anyone could see him out there, and I shook my head as he walked back to the bed.

"What?" he asked, setting his glass down, then filling my wine glass and handing it to me.

"Don't walk on the balcony like that."

His brow shot up.

"Hey, if you can scold me for wearing what I wear, I can scold you for walking out there naked. I already have that trampy manager trying to get in your pants. I don't need to fight the rest of the women in this resort for your attention."

He laughed as he crawled back into bed, taking the wine glass away from me and pinning my arms to the side of my head. "You don't have to fight for my attention. I think I want an appetizer before our dinner gets here."

My stomach flipped, my legs twisting with excitement as he kissed me with an intensity that stirred the flames in me. He continued to ravage me until our dinner came and he ordered them to leave it at the door because he hadn't finished fucking me. I should have scolded him for talking about me like that, but that was Tyson, and it was the comfortable way we were with each other. One that continued to morph with every touch, every moan, and every climax that filled the rest of our night.

By the time we'd completely exhausted ourselves, our dinner was cold again and both of us were too tired to get up. I snuggled into his chest, wondering why it felt so comfortable. I never spent the night with men. There was a line there I didn't want to cross. I took them in back rooms and cars, in the shadowed hallways of clubs, my father's men always blocking entry or standing guard. But I never let one close enough to hold me. Until now. With Tyson it was different and even though our hatred for each other had overshadowed our relationship for years, being in his arms felt right.

"Don't get comfortable, Anj," Tyson grumbled as if he read my thoughts. I adjusted my head to peek up at him. "This is the second time we've shared this bed. I don't like sharing, so don't make it a habit."

I bit his chest, and he grabbed my face, his other hand sinking into my hair and twisting strands into his grip.

"Don't be an asshole," I retorted, wincing as he tugged hard.

"Don't be a cunt," he growled.

"You like that word, Tyson? It comes out of your mouth an

awful lot." The aggressive banter had returned, and I relaxed into the ease of it.

"I normally don't like that word unless I'm using it for you. You bring it out in me."

"Huh, you bring out a stomach-turning bile kind of feeling in me." I tried not to smile and saw the slight twitch of his lip. He was enjoying this as much as I was. Whatever this was that we had, neither of us knew what to do with it.

"Go to sleep, bitch, or I'll make you sleep on the floor," he groused, pushing me off his chest.

"But then you wouldn't have such easy access to my body." I rolled over, turning my back on him and pulling the sheets up higher.

Within seconds, he turned his body into mine, spooning me, his hand coming around to cup my breast. "I can fuck you just as easily on the floor as I can in the bed, Anj. Bend you over and tear you up so much I leave rug burns on those knees."

"Mmm, is that a promise?"

His dick jumped, which was surprising with how many times we'd had sex. The man had a stamina that rivaled any man I'd met, and the thought sent a tingle of currents flooding my body.

"We can try that tomorrow," he said, nibbling my shoulder. "Go to sleep before I toss you out of this bed."

I pushed into him, his hand pulling me even further against his chest, and relaxed into his hold. I listened to his calming breaths as his body spooned mine, thinking of how natural this felt when it shouldn't have. We'd shifted from enemies to lovers quickly and as much as it excited me, worry nagged at the back of my mind. This wasn't us. Two people who cuddled in bed together after sex or even had sex. I chewed the inside of my cheek and covered his hand with mine, unsure of where this was heading and with a nagging suspicion that it was all too good to be true.

Chapter Eleven

TYSON

A ngie was asleep in my arms. I'd held her the entire night as if even in sleep I didn't want her slipping from my grasp. The thought overwhelmed me as I gently disentangled myself from her body, remembering how I'd done the same thing the morning before. She fit so perfectly in my hold, her body molding to mine like we were meant to be together. Rolling over, I stared at the ceiling. This was dangerous, an attachment I didn't want, one I didn't need. I ran my hand through my hair, trying my best not to wake her. She shifted her body like she knew I no longer held her and turned over, curling into me, her hand stretching over my body. The steady rise and fall of her chest let me know she was still asleep, and I took the moment to appreciate how peaceful this was.

Angie brought out a part of me I didn't know how to deal with, one I'd hidden for years, only revealing it to those closest to me. I didn't need attachment, commitment, love. Sex was all I wanted, all I'd told myself I needed.

Taking a strand of her hair, I let my fingers drift along it. I'd wanted Angie. That realization burned through me like a raging fire that scorched the place in my heart that had been hers all these years. Shadowed with my irritation and hatred so that I didn't have to admit it.

And now she was mine. That thought settled too well in my chest and no matter how I tried to push it away, I couldn't. The barriers we'd placed between us had cracked and there was no putting them back in place. No matter how many times we tried.

She nuzzled her face into my chest and kissed it, sending my pulse racing. As if her action worried her, she peeked up at me, a crease between her eyes. I drew my arm around her and pulled her further into me, reassuring her and myself that this was all right, and she relaxed, giving me a fantastic smile.

"Good morning," she said, wiping the sleep from her eyes. I reached my finger over to sweep away the rest.

"It will be once I'm buried deep inside of you."

"You're so romantic," she said, rolling her eyes.

"I don't do romantic, baby." With a push, I moved her from me, hovering over her.

"And what do you do, Tyson?" Her brown eyes were lazy, her fingers trailing up my chest. Every part of me wanted to kiss her and tell her I would do romantic for her, that I would tear down my walls and love her the way I'd always wanted. But those words were still too uncertain, too new and ones I feared saying.

So instead, I draped my tongue down her body before grabbing her hip and flipping her over. With a slap to her ass, I dragged it back and leaned over her. "I do hard and dirty fucking, little viper." A tremble ran through her, and she pushed her ass into me. The regret that I'd turned the moment, hiding my emotions with my desire for her body, nudged at me, but I disregarded it, knowing she was just like me in too many ways. And that this was what we needed, what I needed to make it through.

Skating my fingers down her spine, I bit her ass and slid my thumb through her warmth, feeling the wetness building there.

"Is there any part of this body that's still virgin?" I asked, spreading her arousal up her ass.

She moaned, and I knew from that sound that there wasn't, and my insides clenched with a mix of envy and hunger because I wanted to experience how tight that ass was and to be the first to claim it.

"Damn, Anj. You're such a slut." I gave her another slap, sending her body lurching forward, then sank my fingers into her wetness, loving how soaked she'd grown.

"If I'm a slut, you're a whore," she muttered, throwing her hair back as she brought herself to her hands.

I spread my fingers along her ass crack before pushing through her folds and against her clit, teasing her. "I'd watch that mouth of yours, or I'll take you so hard in this ass you won't sit right the rest of the day." She groaned, and I shoved her head down, thrusting into her, her body shivering in anticipation. But I wasn't ready to destroy her completely. I wanted her to come first. She was already close, and I throbbed at the thought. I grabbed her hips, driving deeper into her. She raised her head, but I shoved her back down, reaching over to touch her breast as I slowed my pace. Rolling her nipple between my fingers, I watched as the trembles started along her body.

Seeing Angie climax was becoming my favorite pastime. She was glorious, and it only sent me further over the cliff the way she fell apart, every inch of her body quaking in ecstasy.

"That's it, baby, come for me." As if I'd summoned it, her climax tore through her, her body spasming around me so tight, I almost lost it with her. "Fuck," I muttered, grabbing her hips and pounding into her again. She felt so good, I never wanted it to stop, but I needed to or I wouldn't be able to take her the way I really wanted, and I wanted to feel that ass around me before I splattered her body with my cum. I couldn't wait to see how she responded to that because, with her insistence that I shower yesterday, I knew she hadn't let anyone come all over her. That was something I was claiming for myself.

Reluctantly, I pulled out, ignoring the complaints from my

body as I pushed my fingers through her arousal and spread it over her before grabbing those hips again and guiding my tip into her ass. She groaned so loud it almost coaxed my orgasm from me, and I lost control of my pacing and plunged into her as I pulled her back to meet my motion. A cry tore from her and I worried for just a minute until she pushed further against me, reaffirming what I'd suspected about my girl. That as prissy and stuck-up as she tried to be, she was just as naughty as I was.

She was so tight that it didn't take long for me to lose it. Just as another climax trembled through her and sent her body clamping down on me, my release hit me like a rogue wave, drowning me as I pulled out and splattered over her back. The sight heightened my release, leaving me so weakened that I collapsed next to her. She picked her head up from where I'd ground it into the sheets when I'd come. Her eyes were mischievous, with a glint of danger in them.

"Did you really just send that shit all over my body?" She looked disgusted, which only caused me to laugh.

"Fuck yeah, that was amazing. And it wasn't all over your body, just your back and..." I picked my head up and looked her over, loving how sexy she looked with my cum on her. "And now it's dripping down your ass crack, which I just owned."

"You're a bastard, Tyson."

"Just marking my territory, baby. That ass is mine now."

Her eyes lit and I instinctively hardened myself to it, knowing what those words implied and not liking how it sounded. I snapped my hand through my hair and left the bed, heading to the bathroom.

"I should make you leave the room with my cum all over you," I said, turning the shower on.

"I don't think so, shithead. And don't think about marking me again." She pushed me aside, trying to look tough, but I could see the quake in her legs.

142

Biting back my smile, I replied, "I'll mark you any time I want, little viper, and you'll like it every time."

"That's what you think."

"Just wait until I coat those tits and that face, Anj."

She hissed, the sound calling to me like a mating call.

We had returned to the back and forth that defined us and it was a place I liked, one I suspected she welcomed just like I did. She met my eyes as she smoothed the water through her hair, and they revealed more than I thought she wanted me to see. They were shining a light amber, emotion clear in them, an emotion I was having trouble denying but one I wanted to run from. Love.

MY PHONE RANG as I was watching Angie comb the wet tangles out of her hair. I was looking forward to seeing how sexy she'd look when her natural color grew in, and I wondered at that certain anticipation. She had put on a short jumper that hugged her ass too perfectly and rose up her thighs every time she moved the brush through her hair. There was no back to it, the front gathering in a V like the dress she'd worn the night before, her tits sitting perfectly bare below the material. The sight of her had me salivating until the thought occurred to me that other men would look at her the same way. A jolt of jealousy ripped through me like the sting of a blade.

"You're not wearing that out," I told her, picking up my phone.

"Who made you my boss?" she snapped without looking over at me. "I don't remember the word 'daddy' coming from these lips."

"I remember coming between those lips."

This time, she did look over at me.

"Keep it up and that will be the last time."

"Give me a second, Mace," I said, answering the call. I put the phone down and strutted over to her.

A twist of my hand in her wet hair had her body against mine and her eyes flaring with desire. "Change the fucking outfit and cover that body up so I don't have to kill every man here."

I shoved her away and walked back to the phone. "I'm going to walk my irritation off before I grab us some coffee. By the time I get back, I expect you to have changed."

"Screw you, Tyson," she muttered as I put the phone to my ear.

"Don't make me spank you again, Anj. I won't go gentle on you this time."

I walked out, hearing her swear and shaking my head as I passed Finch and one of Donelli's men. Finch followed me, always vigilant, and I heard Donelli's guy call his partner to back him up.

"What's up, Mace?" I asked, heading further down the hall.

"Going well, huh?"

"Something like that." I couldn't keep up the gruff mask with Mason. He'd read right through it. And he knew me too well not to notice.

"What's wrong, Ty?"

I eyed the elevator and decided to take the stairs, wanting the privacy. Finch followed, but I motioned for him to give me some space. He moved past me, checking out the rest of the stairwell.

"Why do you ask?" I ran my hand through my hair as I leaned against the wall.

"Because you're not bitching about Angie Donelli. I thought she was a pain in your ass."

"She is," I said, my eyes staring at the step in front of me. "She's a bratty, spoiled bitch who drives me insane. Everything she does grates on my nerves and pretending like this is killing me, Mace. I don't think I can take much more of it."

"But?" he asked, reading me easily because the usual aggression in my tone was missing.

"But...she's making me crazy." I sighed.

"Ty, that picture you sent for Joey...that wasn't staged, was it?"

I heard Casey in the background, her voice growing a pitch higher with excitement. Damn, I should have known she'd be with him.

"No." I slid onto the stair. "No, it wasn't. Shit, Mace, I can't keep my hands off her. It built up, you know, this craving inside of me I couldn't stop until I had her. And now, it's like I can't stop and...I don't know that I want to stop because she does something to me, makes me so..." I paused, unable to get the words out.

"You're in love with Angie Donelli?" his voice was incredulous, but it was Casey's surprised scream that made me smile. The word was one I hadn't wanted to admit, but when he said it, I couldn't deny it.

"Yeah, I think I am. Completely and utterly in love with the bitch who has made my life miserable for the last seven years."

"We can have a double wedding!" Casey yelled.

"No!" What was she thinking even saying that? But something about it had sounded right, and I shook the sensation off. "No. What the fuck, Mason? Calm her down."

"Oh, you don't want me to do that, buddy. You won't like the way I calm her down."

I rolled my eyes, wanting to reach through the phone and strangle him.

"So, did you tell her yet?" Casey said, having clearly grabbed the phone from Mason.

"Case, settle down. And no, I haven't. We...this is all new for both of us, and I don't even know if she feels the same way." But I did. I'd seen the look in her eyes that she'd shielded quickly.

"You need to tell her, Ty. This is huge. For both of you!"

"Yeah, it is, Case, which is why I'm not gonna say anything yet. I'm not ready and I'm not even sure what it is I'm feeling."

"Give me the damn phone, princess, or I'll tie you up with that scarf—"

"Mason," I scolded, not wanting to hear anymore.

That stupid purple scarf that he carried in his pocket now drove me nuts. It was from the set Casey and I had split and I didn't like the thought of them using my mother's scarf in their sex games. I had a few of my own tucked in my closet, not sure what to do with them. When I'd caught Angie sleeping in my bed, she'd had the blue one clutched in her hands. It had pissed me off that she'd gone through my things, but seeing her like that had soothed the irritation.

"Fine. Go enjoy more of your wife."

"I will," I replied, thinking of all the ways I wanted to enjoy Angie today, a surprising few not sexual. "Hey, what is Casey doing there? I thought you were meeting with Tirenti still?"

"I brought her with me. She's cleaning out her apartment. I'm going back to see Tirenti with Donelli later. They're negotiating and I'm mediating. Now that Angie's out of the picture, Tirenti wants more in trade from Donelli. I'm still suspicious that he's thinking of turning."

"Be careful and make sure you go well armed."

"Got it. You keep that prize busy while I turn Joey's attention to something else."

He disconnected, and I sat in the stairwell for a few more minutes, thinking about Angie and how I felt about her. As much as she aggravated me, I'd fallen for her. I had fallen for her that first time I'd seen her years ago, but now I was lost to her. And as much as I hated to admit that a woman had claimed my heart and destroyed the guardrails I had in place around it, I couldn't deny that Angie had done just that. She had elbowed her way into my heart, one foul-mouthed remark after another. And the hate that had sat between us had been nothing but a shield to my attraction to her. It had taken only a few days alone with her to realize it. Years of hiding from it, of denying how like a vine that overtakes a fence, she had rooted herself into my consciousness, into my very being and I'd refused to recognize it.

Deciding I needed to get some fresh air before I returned to her, I went for a walk, using the back entrance to the resort to avoid the bustle of the front lobby. I needed to prepare myself mentally, knowing when I saw Angie next, I was going to dismantle those guardrails completely and tell her how I really felt.

Chapter Twelve

ANGIE

Tyson left the room, not heeding my complaints about changing. I didn't know who he thought he was, telling me what to wear. But as angry as it made me, part of me liked it because that insistence that I cover myself more was revealing. He'd never cared before, only making snide comments about how easy I was. But now, his behavior was possessive, and it made my insides tumble around.

That sensation grew as I thought about how he'd taken me earlier, bringing my body to life like he did every time he touched me. Like no man ever had. And I knew no other man would because Tyson's touch burned through me, marking me just like he'd said.

When I'd met his eyes, my heart had leaped so hard it thudded against my chest and I recognized the sensation. It was one I'd avoided for years, one I didn't want because it hurt so much. But his eyes had shone with that same emotion, the hues in them sparkling before he turned from me. Love. The one emotion both of us ran from, seeking to numb our hearts with random sex and meaningless hook-ups. Men I'd taken to dull the strange ache that sat in my chest every time I saw him. It wasn't often. His visits were quick, but each time that ache grew like an annoyance I couldn't shake, one I couldn't understand.

I set my brush down, thinking of how this time had changed us, changed me. Intensifying what had been there and electrifying it. Love. I was in love with Tyson Raines and the thought of our fake marriage ending, of returning to Armina alone, without him, hurt so badly that I shoved the thought aside. I didn't want this to end because I needed his touch now. Craved it so that I knew I couldn't live without it. He'd ruined me for every other man.

My heart pounded as I threw open the door, needing to tell him, to hear him say those words back to me and to reassure me that I'd ruined him, too, and he wouldn't let me go home. That he'd steal me from my life and keep me by his side, touching and loving me forever.

"Where did he go?" I asked Ben, the guard my father had sent with me. My mind was a cacophony of emotion that was about to erupt. Maybe I was being childish, but the need to tell him I loved him burned through me, driving me toward him.

"He took the stairs. What's wrong, Angie?"

Ignoring him, I hobbled down the hall, cursing my damned ankle. I pushed the door to the stairs open, catching it before it slammed. *Get a grip,* I scolded myself, not wanting to look like a madwoman. I smoothed my hand down my jumper to calm the nerves that were suddenly pummeling me, hearing words from further down the stairs that stopped me in my track.

"She's a bratty, spoiled bitch who drives me insane. Everything she does grates on my nerves and pretending like this is killing me, Mace. I don't think I can take much more of it."

My heart dropped and my hands shook as I backed out of the stairwell and quietly closed the door, standing there frozen. The words played over and over in my head. Pretending. That's all he was doing? Pretending to want me. Playing with me, with my body, with my heart. A strange bubble built inside of my chest like a wave that needed to escape, and I opened my mouth as I backed further away, a sob coming from me. It was a sound I hadn't heard since my mother died, because I hadn't cried since that day. Nothing had ever brought me as much pain. Until now.

Devastated, I returned to the room, the warm tears burning my skin, unwelcome and unwanted, a show of weakness that I couldn't stop. Doubling over, I dropped to the floor, hating that I'd been so vulnerable, that I'd fallen for his game, that I'd opened my heart when I'd kept it guarded for so long. Every small gesture, every tender moment played through my mind, arguing that this couldn't be, that he couldn't have played me. But he had. His words were confirmation.

Anger burned through me, and I embraced it, burying the hurt, the ache that was shredding me from the inside out. No one played me. I was Angela Donelli, not some foolish little girl. I stood, wiping the tears from my face, and limped to the bathroom. I started tossing my things into my bag until I caught sight of myself in the mirror. No one made me cry, and this man had done that.

"You're a stupid fool, Angie. Hate him, despise him, but never love." I grabbed my makeup and covered my freckles, then my birthmark, erasing the parts of me he'd lied to me about. When I'd finished, I threw the rest of my stuff in the bag and started packing my suitcases, letting my rage cover the ache that wouldn't ease in my chest.

The door opened, Tyson's cheerful voice entering before he did, "I had them use that fancy almond..." He stopped, but I didn't look at him. It hurt too much. I'd wanted to be packed before he returned. "Angie?"

"I'm leaving. You don't have to pretend anymore. I'll deal with Joey."

"Angie, what are you talking about?"

I ignored him, closing my case and zipping it. He grabbed me, turning me toward him. "What are you talking about?"

I jerked out of his grasp. "You're an asshole, Tyson Raines. You didn't have to do what you did. To use me that way."

"Use you, baby? What are—"

"Don't call me that!" I snapped, grabbing my bag. "I hate you, Tyson. I've always hated you and I will curse your name on my deathbed. Find me a way home, now."

"Angela, I don't know what's gotten into you, but—" The confused and hurt look on his face confused me, and I stumbled, the pain in my ankle overtaking the pain in my heart.

He reached out to steady me.

"Don't touch me," I said, stepping away and hearing my voice crack. "Never touch me again. We hate each other, that's it, that's all this has ever been. Your game is over."

"What game?" I could see the confusion turning to anger, his temper rising.

"Me. I was your game all this time. And I fell for it, like an idiot. Damn you, Tyson. You only had to put up with me, pretend we were married. You didn't have to touch me. What was that for? Why bother? So you can go back and tell Mason what an annoying bitch I was to screw?"

The darkness returned to his eyes, his expression turning hard. "You are an annoying bitch, Angie. You've always been."

"Yeah, so I heard. Well, you don't have to pretend and put up with me anymore. I don't want to be an inconvenience to you and your dick."

His eyes widened. "Shit, you were listening in on my conversation with Mason. What did you hear?"

That unpleasant sensation in my chest returned. "Enough." I yanked the rings from my finger and threw them at him. He caught them and looked down at them. "I don't need you, Tyson. I never did."

He clenched his hand around the rings, the glimmer of hurt reflected in his eyes morphing to anger. "Good, because I'm tired of you, Angie. Get out. I'll have a plane ready, and you can return to Joey Tirenti." He let the rings fall, taking his off and throwing it to the floor. "Let him put up with your spoiled ass. I'm sure he'll fuck you the way you want it. Just make sure you take your makeup with you. You'll need it to cover the bruises...if you're still alive when he's done with you."

"Prick," I spat.

"Yeah, that's what I am, Angie. A prick. And you're a bitch who deserves everything you have coming to you."

I smacked him, the pain so intense I couldn't hold back. He grabbed my wrist, squeezing it painfully, and slammed me into the door, which shook on its hinges.

"You touch me again and I'll send your body back in pieces to your father," he snarled. "It'll be better than what he'll get when Tirenti's done with you."

With a shove, he walked away, turning his back on me and running his hand through his hair. I grabbed my bag and left, the tears pushing against my hold on them.

"Get her dumb ass on a plane. I think the governor is leaving this morning. Maybe she can give his spoiled son a blow job on the way, maybe ride the governor while she's at it," Tyson ordered.

I stepped onto the elevator, staring ahead and not looking at his henchman or mine. All I could do was let the hatred for Tyson fester in my chest to coat the agony that was setting in. There was nothing more to do. I was shattered, uncertain for the first time in my life. I'd fallen in love with him, thinking he loved me, too. But it hadn't been love, it had all been fake, and that realization crippled me.

I tried building my defenses back as Tyson's man talked to the governor, who was waiting for his luggage to be loaded into a car. I'd timed my leave just right, it seemed. He made his way back over.

"They'll take you to Armina before they return home."

"Thank you," I mumbled, trying to firm the shake in my voice.

"Can I ask you something?" he said, as I walked away.

"Sure."

"What did you hear before you came back to the room? What did the boss say?"

I considered whether it was worth telling him, whether it mattered now. "Just the usual. What a spoiled brat I am and how it was killing him to be stuck with me, pretending to like me. Nothing different from the usual."

He looked like he wanted to reply, but I turned from him, not wanting to hear any excuses. Tyson didn't deserve them.

THE FLIGHT BACK WAS QUIET. I stayed in the back of the plane, ignoring the family, their stares, the questions in their eyes. A car was waiting for me when I returned and I knew Tyson had let my father know the sham was over, that I'd walked away. And I knew what it meant—that I'd have to deal with Joey and his self-imposed claim over me. The thought was terrifying, especially after learning how he treated his women. My father would have no choice, though. To keep his hold on the territory, I would be the chess piece he sacrificed. Without Tyson's claim, Mason had no say in this part of the relationship between my father and Tirenti.

"Well, well. If it isn't my future wife," Joey said as I exited the car.

"What are you doing here, Joey? And why are your creepily stalking outside my home?"

He gave me a smirk, my body's response nothing like it was to the smirks Tyson gave me.

"My father and I had a meeting here today but with the news that you left Raines, the meeting disbanded and I stayed to claim my prize."

I walked past him. "I'm not your prize."

Grabbing my wrist, he stopped me. "Yes, you are. Raines gave you up, although it seems you let him touch that body before he did. That picture he sent is still in my phone, and I can't tell you how many times I've jerked off to your sexy ass."

"That's gross." I tried to pull away, but he held me steady. My ankle was hurting again, so I shifted my weight, tumbling toward him a little.

"Get your hands off my sister," Tony commanded, storming out of the house.

"I can touch her all I want now. She's mine and she's coming home with me."

Tony's jaw clenched, his fists bunching, and I knew he was trying not to punch Joey. He jerked me from Joey's hold, my ankle giving out when he unbalanced me. "Did Raines hurt you?" he asked, steadying me.

"No, I twisted my ankle," I snapped, not wanting to talk about it. "What does he mean I'm going with him?"

"Let me talk to my sister," Tony said. "She needs to see my father, too. You can wait out here."

He ushered me into the house, not saying anything further.

"Tony, what is going on?" I asked, exhausted from the emotional day I'd had.

"What did you do to ruin things with Raines?" he asked, pushing me into my father's office.

"I didn't do anything. He did." My voice trembled. The wall I'd built to keep the pain and tears at bay broke, and I collapsed into his arms. My brother had always been my rock, the only one who saw my vulnerable side, even if I kept it from him most of the time.

He embraced me, soothing my hair with his hand as the tears wracked my body. "Anj, what happened?" he asked, worry lining his voice. "Do I need to hunt that prick down and kill him?"

I shook my head against his chest. "No. He's just an asshole and I let my guard down."

He pushed me back. "Did that asshole touch you?"

"Shut up, Joey. Men touch me all the time and you never give two shits about it."

"The hell I don't. I hate that you sleep around, sis. I want to kill every man who touches you because you're my little sister. But if Raines touched you—"

"You won't do anything."

His brow creased as he studied me. "Something happened, didn't it?"

"Go away, Tony. Let me see Dad."

"No," he said, pushing me back in front of him and holding my shoulders. "Tell me what went down, Anj."

"You don't need to know."

"Yes, I do because that twat out there is about to take you to his territory and marry you now that Raines is out of the way."

My mouth dropped, my knees trembling. "He can't."

"Yes, he can. He doesn't give a shit about the marriage to Raines and he didn't believe it in the first place. With the sham blown up, Mason didn't have any choice but to concede to step out and let Dad and Tirenti handle it. He left this morning. Dad's hands are tied. He and Mason suspect Tirenti is being swayed by the Bad Omen and the only thing that can stop that is a union between the two families."

"Me and Joey."

"Yeah," he said, confirming my suspicions about what I faced when I turned my back on Tyson. "Now tell me what happened with Raines."

My mind was going through so many thoughts that it was hard to find the words. I didn't want to marry Joey. As much as I'd talked a good game when I'd been angry with Tyson, I didn't want to be anywhere near Joey. He terrified me.

"I...he...we..."

"Spit it out, Anj. Did he touch you?"

"Yes."

His anger boiled over, his hands clenching into my shoulders.

"But I wanted him to. It was consensual." I shrugged his hands away and leaned against the closest chair, trying to rest my ankle. "I love him, Tony. And he hurt me."

His face softened, then morphed back to anger. "He hurt you? I'll fuck him up so bad—"

"No, don't. It was my fault. I let my guard down and I thought... I thought he was falling, that he wasn't pretending, and he was. The entire time."

"He slept with you as part of the sham marriage thing? That doesn't make sense, Anj. He hates you and you...well I thought you hated him, but apparently not."

I chuckled, thinking about his words. "But I heard him. He said he was tired of pretending, and that I was just a spoiled brat and being with me was killing him."

Tony tipped his head. "Anj, what did you do when you heard that?"

"I left. We had a big fight, and I left him."

He swiped his hand down his face.

"Time's up, Angie. We're leaving," Joey barged into the office.

"Leaving?" I asked Tony.

He nodded. "You're going with him. He wants a wedding asap. Tomorrow."

This time, my jaw hit the floor. "Tomorrow?"

"Tomorrow, baby," Joey said.

"Don't call me that," I snapped, the word cleaving my heart.

"I'll call you anything you want when I'm owning that hot body of yours."

Tony turned on him, grabbing him by the collar and shoving him against the wall. His men pulled their guns, as did ours. "You talk about my sister like that again, and I'll break both your legs before I cut your cock off."

"Enough!" my father's voice boomed from the hallway.

Tony released Joey, who indignantly brushed at his suit. My father walked into the room, followed by Tirenti.

"Angela." My father came over and gave me a kiss on the cheek, but I could see the disappointment in his eyes. I'd messed this up, put him in a bad spot, and now we were both paying the price.

"Hi, Daddy," I said, unable to disguise the guilt that sat heavy on me.

"Your father and I have come to an agreement," Tirenti said. "We'll hold the wedding here tomorrow. His attorneys are working on annulling the marriage to Raines as we speak."

I dropped my eyes, sensing Joey move next to me. His arm came around me and I cringed instinctively.

"Tomorrow still? I can't wait to become part of the family," he said, squeezing my arm.

"Tomorrow afternoon," my father confirmed, his sight on Joey's hands.

"But Daddy—"

"No, Angela. The decision has been made." His eyes narrowed, anger in them, and my father was never angry at me. "Leave us, all of you. Tony, please show our guests and their men out."

He kept his eyes on me, the proud man I respected not giving the conniving ass behind him a second glass, nor his son, for that matter. We both waited until the door closed.

"Daddy—"

"What did you do, Angela?" His expression was stony, and it hurt.

"I didn't do anything."

"No? Then why are you out of his protection? Do you have any idea what you've done?"

"He hurt me." I heard the weakness in my voice, the fear behind it because my father never took his anger out on me.

"What did he do? Did he hit you? Touch you wrong?" He moved closer, looking me over, concern in his eyes.

"No, he didn't do anything like that."

"Then you should have stayed, because whatever he did is better than what Joey Tirenti will do." The hardness in his features softened, a look of defeat taking over him. "I tried to protect you, Angela. Gave you to Raines in desperation, but now...now I can no longer protect you. With Raines involved, Joey would have lost interest, moved to his next victim, but with him no longer in the picture, you're his for the taking." He sighed, a long, pained sound that said all he needed about how much he'd fought to keep me safe. "I'm not in the position to fight him, and your brother is too green. His interests have only now turned to the family business."

"But Mason—"

"No, Mason has stepped out of this. It's between the families in our province and Mason's hold on Tirenti is old and it's slipping. The Bad Omen have been working Tirenti, wearing him down, and now that Mason and Tides are aligned, Tirenti's allegiance has shifted. Tirenti hates Tides. It's a rift that goes back to before you were born, and one that even Mason can't fix."

I leaned against the desk, realization setting in that I'd done this, making a hasty move, a decision fueled by my emotion. I'd confronted Tyson and pushed him, and he'd sent me away. But I'd always confronted him, always bit back, always pushed his buttons, and he'd never turned away.

"You will marry Joey Tirenti and mend the divide to keep your brother and the family safe," he said, pulling me from the thought.

He moved closer to me, rubbing his thumb over my cheek and giving me a sad smile. "I miss your freckles," he said as he rubbed my makeup away. "You look so much like your mother, no matter how you try to hide it."

Tears pooled in my eyes, and I fought my hold on them. "I'm sorry, Daddy."

"I know, sweetheart. I just wish I could fight this, but if I do, I'll lose you both. Tirenti has promised me no harm will come to you, and I have no choice but to trust him."

I nodded, hating that I was a pawn in this war. A pawn that had passed from one player to another, one who would never give me what Tyson had, never touch me like he had, never appreciate the real me, and one I would never love. Not like I loved Tyson, no matter how much my heart was breaking because of it.

Standing, I held my head high, putting my usual façade on. "I'll need my nails done and my hair."

"It's just a small ceremony, Angela. Just to make it official."

I grimaced at the thought. "It's my wedding day. I want to look pretty. And I want to spend my last night here. Not with Joey. He can wait one more day before his slimy hands touch me."

"Whatever you want, sweetheart."

He gave me a kiss on the head, squeezing my hand before leaving the room. I remained there, my grip on the desk steadying me because if I didn't hold tight, I would collapse. How had my life turned upside down so quickly? I'd gone from the safety of Tyson's arms to a tightrope that would send us all tumbling to our doom if I made the wrong move. The family business had never been my concern, but now it had become mine to protect and no matter how terrified that thought made me, I had no choice but to accept the fate I'd set in front of me when I'd run from the only man who could have protected me.

Chapter Thirteen

TYSON

The door stayed closed. Angie didn't return. Yet I stood there, frozen and unable to make myself move. My mind was trying to process what had happened. How we'd gone from a morning of amazing sex and tender moments that had left me ready to bare my soul to her, to experiencing the shallow emptiness that now consumed my body. I didn't understand what she was talking about. Why she'd been so angry with me, so hurt.

She'd overheard me in the hall, but I'd been saying good things, talking about admitting my emotions. Something I'd been planning to do when I'd walked in the door, opening my heart to her, to what I'd denied all this time. I sat on the bed, staring at the rings on the floor and trying to figure out how it had all gone wrong.

Finch came in and tried talking to me, but I put my hand out to stop him, not ready to talk yet. I was still too empty. He left me alone with the shake of his head. Running my hands through my hair, I walked onto the balcony, trying not to think of Angie, of how we'd sat there together, how soft her legs had been in my lap, the way the sun had shimmered in her hair.

I pulled my phone out, knowing I needed to warn Mason, to let him know I'd screwed up and let her walk out. That I'd just sent her to swim with the sharks.

"Hey," he answered. "How'd it go?"

"Are you with Donelli yet?" I asked, disregarding his question.

"I'm on my way. Tirenti is en route. Why?"

I sat, staring out at the beach. "Because I fucked up...I'm not really sure how, but I lost her."

"You what?" he yelled into the phone. "How did you lose her on an island that small?"

"Not like that, asshole. She left. Something upset her and we had a fight, and she walked out."

"And you just let her go?" I could hear the anger in his voice, his teeth grinding while he awaited my answer.

"I may have kicked her out, but in my defense, she was packing when I returned to the room."

"Shit, Ty. I thought you were in love. What happened to that in the short time since we talked?"

I leaned on my knees, wishing I had the answer. "I don't know. I seriously don't."

There was a knock on the door, so I rose, saying to Mason, "Let Donelli know. She doesn't want my protection anymore. She made that clear. The sham is up and I'm out."

"That means Tirenti is his problem to deal with," he said. "Without us in the middle, it's a territory thing, and Donelli isn't in the position to keep Angie safe without starting a war."

I opened the door to Finch and ushered him in. I could see he was still eager to tell me something.

"And if it's a war, Donelli will lose," I said.

"Exactly. I'll warn Donelli before Tirenti comes and we'll come up with something."

"For Angie's sake, I hope you do," I said, hanging up. The thought of Joey Tirenti getting his hands on her was enough to make me see red.

Finch had been waiting patiently for me, and I signaled for him to talk.

"I delivered the package. The governor took her."

"Thanks, Finch."

I expected him to leave, but he lingered.

"Don't take this the wrong way..." My jaw ticked just at his words, and I waited for him to continue. "...but you have a tendency to leap before you look."

"What's that supposed to mean?"

"I've worked with you and Mason long enough to know how you two behave. I'm just saying, I don't think you listened to what she was telling you."

"And how do you know that? Were you in here when she was packing her bags and telling me she hated me?"

He snorted. "No, but I heard it all. Besides, she tells you she hates you all the time. Since when does that bother you?"

I shoved my phone in my pocket and looked away, knowing he was right. It had bothered me this time when it never had before because I'd expected to pull her into my arms and tell her how I felt, to kiss her and spend the day with her. But her reaction when I'd entered put me on the defensive and once I was there, it was difficult to pull me back.

"She made it clear she wanted to leave and never see me again. It's over and it should never have begun."

"It's over because you didn't stop to ask her why she was upset. I don't think she heard your entire conversation, boss."

My eyes shot up at him as the memory of her words returned, the way they'd focused on only certain words I'd told Mason. That I was tired of pretending, that she was a brat, and it was killing me to be with her.

"Fuck," I muttered, a sense of defeat making my shoulders slump. She wasn't leaving because I'd gotten too close, she was leaving because she had, and she thought none of it was real to me. That I'd used her. "Get me a car."

He raised a brow.

"Get me a car now and get me to the airport!" An urgency took over my body, a need to get to her before she got on that plane because if I didn't, there was no getting her back. I thought about calling Mason while Finch called about a car, but I needed to talk to Angie first. If I couldn't convince her to listen to me, then it wouldn't matter that I'd discovered the miscommunication.

It never occurred to me that I wouldn't make it on time, that I wouldn't see her again. But when the car finally pulled up to the small airport after the longest ride I'd ever endured, the plane was taxiing. Finch sped, the car screeching onto the airstrip just as its wheels lifted. A pain like I'd never experienced wrenched its way into my chest as Finch stopped the car. Fumbling with the handle, my hands shaking, I burst from the car, running after the plane as if I could stop it myself. Her name tore from my throat, a gut-wrenching sound that left me so fractured I could only stare as the plane grew further away.

She was gone, out of my reach and stubbornly thinking this had been nothing more than the fake relationship it started as. And the fact that she'd acted that way, that she'd been so reactive, so hurt, told me she'd fallen just as hard as I had. That recognition didn't ease my pain because I knew she was hurting. And I knew she would hide it, burn it away with her anger, just as I had when she'd turned on me.

In one more act of desperation, I pulled my phone out and tried calling her, the call going to voicemail just like I'd suspected it would. I didn't bother to leave a message. She was too stubborn to listen to any messages I left. In her mind, it was over. I'd used her and hurt her and nothing I said would erase that. She would shield the pain and use her anger to function. Because Angie was the mirror to me and that's exactly what I would have done. It was what I'd done in the hotel room when I'd thrown her out. When I'd made the worst mistake of my life.

THE BURN of the alcohol didn't help to burn away the ache that sat in my chest or the void of not having Angie near me. It seemed unreal that in only two days she'd cracked my defenses and released the heart that had been hers for the taking all these years. No matter how I tried, I couldn't seem to put it back together because it still belonged to her.

"Your wife took off without you." I raised my head to see the sexy resort manager standing next to me. "Her loss."

The tight skirt and form fitting button down with the top buttons strategically left undone would have tempted me in the past, but now that I'd had a taste of Angie, I didn't think anything could tempt me again.

"Don't you have a job? What do we pay you to do every day? Because I don't remember flirting with the guests in your contract."

I turned back to my glass and took another swig.

"I don't flirt with the guests, just you." Shit, I would have broken Mason's rule just to numb the pain, but I didn't think it would do the trick. Besides, I could just hear Angie's wrath if I so much as looked at the woman again and if I slept with her and she found out, there would be no coming back from that. Not that I thought there was any coming back as it stood.

I glanced over at her, and she licked her dark red lips, a move that normally would have had me accepting her offer.

"I can take your mind from her." She was good, and my impulsive dick lurched a little.

"I don't think I want my mind off her and I'm not happy you assumed I do. Now turn your sweet ass around and do your job, or we'll find someone who can do it for you."

She huffed away, and I returned to my drink. I needed to talk to Mason about why we insisted on hiring sexy women. I was sure if I brought Casey in on the conversation, there'd be some changes. They were too tempting.

Not that anything was tempting me today. Angie had ruined me and all I wanted was her. It was a thought that left me devastated. My phone rang, and I looked down to see Mason's name flash on the screen.

"Casey and I are home," he said.

"Home? Already?" It had only been a few hours since we'd spoken. I'd spent the morning staring at the pink suitcases on the bed that Angie had left in her haste before I'd turned to the bar to numb the relentless burning in my chest.

"Angie called Donelli and told him she left you. Without you, there's no way he can decline Tirenti's offer to marry her off to Joey."

I gripped the phone, my nerves on edge. "Marry?"

"Yeah, Joey wants her, and Tirenti wants to use it to tighten his hold on the territory. He knows Donelli isn't what he used to be and that Tony's been playing around all these years not paying attention to how to run things. He has Donelli's hands tied, and so I backed out. Without you in the picture, I'm out of the talks. This is between the two of them now."

"But if he marries her, he'll run Donelli down." Just saying the word was like a dull knife repeatedly tearing into my heart.

"No. He knows I've got Donelli's back and Tides has mine. He won't mess with Donelli, but having Angie gives him leverage."

I pulled at my hair, resting my head in my hand. "Joey's a monster, Mace." The thought of his slimy hands on her had me sick. He would hurt her. He wouldn't appreciate her smart mouth, or her witty comebacks, the insults she threw that caused my balls to clench. He would hit her and bruise her delicate features, punching away the things that I loved about her until she was no longer the woman I'd fallen for.

"I know, and Tirenti knows that. If she marries Joey, Donelli will do anything to keep her safe. He'd sell his soul to Tirenti, which is what he's basically doing by letting him have her."

"A bargaining chip to keep them both alive? But being with Joey will kill her. If he doesn't physically do it, he'll wear her spirit down until she's lost."

"Damn, you've got it bad, Ty. I always wondered if that irritation at her wasn't hiding something. Especially when you got that viper tat."

"Shut up, Mace. This is serious."

He sighed, and I sensed his frustration running as deep as mine did. As much as we held rule over several families outside our province, that rule was always situated on a house of cards. We were hours away from the three bosses in Armina. They could turn on us at any time, which was why we always took precautions, keeping men undercover in their territories, monitoring their dealings, and always doubling down on security when we were there. Donelli was the only one we trusted but with Tirenti pressuring him, there was a chance he would waiver, especially if his only daughter was involved.

By now I had paid my tab and walked out of the resort, Finch and Creek with me. "So Tirenti and Donelli work out an agreement, Tirenti gets Angie, Donelli thinks Tirenti will keep her safe from his deranged son and not touch Tony. What's in it for Tirenti?"

"A stronger hold on the territory," Mason answered.

I kicked the sand with my shoe, watching how the grains scattered as they fell. "No, he's up to something. I don't think he gives a shit about Angie. He's just making his son happy and giving him a new pet." I clenched my teeth at the thought.

"What are you thinking?"

"That he's turning on us." We'd suspected, but Tirenti was an old school boss like Tides. He took his time. His patience wasn't at the level of Tides, but he wasn't one to rush. "He'll hit Donelli when he's down and let the Bad Omen walk right into the province. With Donelli out of the picture, he and the Omens rule the bulk of the territory and Strint, no matter how strong his family is, won't stand a chance."

"The Omens then have a stronghold on the west coast," he mused.

"One that rivals the one we have now that Tides is on our side."

He was angry, but I could also sense him thinking it through. Mason was sharp and there weren't many bosses as smart as he was, as calculating, which was why the others feared him, even when we were young. "I'm sending the plane to bring you home. In the meantime, let me see if I can reach Donelli. It's too late to save Angie, but I might be able to warn him to watch his back."

The phone remained to my ear long after he'd hung up. Those words, that it was too late to save Angie, fell like lead on my shoulders. I had no way to reach her, no way to unravel the words spoken between us. The tide was drifting outward, the water pulling the sand back with each wave, and I sat, thinking of how the tide was like fate, pulling Angie away from me bit by bit.

RETURNING HOME DID nothing to ease the absence of Angie's presence. Each step toward the door reminded me of the first night I'd brought her there. I dropped my bag at the door and walked into the kitchen, only to find Mason drilling into my sister, half her clothes off and his still on.

"What the hell, you two," I complained, covering my eyes from my sister's body and turning back around and leaving the room. "Dammit, Case, put some clothes on!"

"Didn't expect you home yet, bud," Mason called, his breathing labored. "Go unpack and let me finish my dinner."

"You're an asshole, Mace!" I walked faster, not wanting to be anywhere near him when he was touching my sister that way. And I definitely didn't want to be close when they finished. The thought of him making my sister orgasm was revolting and anger inducing.

I trudged to my room, throwing my suitcase in the corner, my eyes falling to the spot on the bed where Angie had slept that first night. The scarf she'd found in my closet was still in the spot. Its presence was comforting, and I picked it up, smelling her perfume on it. The smell drifted through my senses, causing a pang in my chest. Still, I wrapped it around my hand and held onto it. The idea of having it close was like being close to her.

The bed looked inviting, but I didn't think there was any way I could sleep. My mind was too alive with thoughts of all that had happened. Instead, I changed into my gym clothes, heading back out just as Mason was coming down the hall.

"Where's Casey?" I asked, throwing him dagger eyes. "You keep that shit to your bedroom, asshole. I don't want to see that."

He shrugged, giving me a smug grin. "She's too sexy to resist."

I punched him, and he rubbed his jaw.

"Don't say shit like that around me. I'm going to the gym to take my anger out on the bags and not your face."

I pushed past him.

"Thought you might want to know the wedding is tomorrow."

My feet faltered, stopping me in my tracks.

"Donelli sent me an invitation."

Turning, I stalked back to him and snatched the phone from him. A plain black and white invitation announcing the marriage of Angela Rosallina Donelli to Joseph Luca Tirenti at one o'clock the next day was staring starkly back at me.

"Is this some kind of joke?" I asked him. "Nobody gets married that fast and Angie would never go for that."

"She would if her father didn't give her a choice, and I'm sure Tirenti pressured him into moving fast."

"But we're not even divorced yet."

He raised a brow. "You were never married, Ty."

"I know," I said, rubbing my face and hating how depressed my voice had sounded when the words had slipped free. "It's just they think we were and that would mean a normal course of separation before she can marry again."

"Different province and Tirenti wants it annulled. Donelli owns the cops and the courts in that territory, so naturally, Tirenti would know he can pull off an annulment in record time. I'm sure Donelli countered that point, but Tirenti is too corrupt to go for it."

"Why so fast?" I was having a hard time comprehending it. Just this morning, I'd been taking Angie hard, reveling in the sound of her moans and the pleasure of her body. How could she be marrying that asshole a day later?

"I think you're right. Tirenti's up to something. It's like he wants Angie far from Donelli and quickly."

"Like he knows Donelli's going down?"

"Maybe."

I looked at him, seeing the concern etched on his features. The invitation on the phone was still sitting there, a reminder of what I'd let slip through my fingers.

"I need to hit something, and Casey will kick my ass if I hit you." I looked around. "Where is she, anyway?"

He gave me a guilty grin. "She went to clean up. I told her she should walk down to see you with my cum dripping from her just to irritate you, but she said she'd cut me off the rest of the night if I even thought about it."

"You're a real shithead. I don't know why I keep hanging out with you." I tossed the phone at him, his laughter trailing me out of the house.

I spent the next few hours pounding my fists until they were raw, my body was drenched with sweat, and the gym had closed. It was mine, so I could have stayed there the entire night, but I knew I needed to return. No matter how much I tried to punch the image of Angie leaving from my mind, I couldn't erase it. The more I punched, the worse it became. Images of her smile, her body, her eyes, plagued me until I finally gave up.

Mason and Casey were nowhere to be found by the time I walked into the house. Grabbing a bottle of water, I made my way to my room, ignoring the scarf on the bed until I'd showered. I sat in the chair across from my bed, my eyes fixed on it. Midnight had come and gone, but I wasn't ready to sleep. I didn't even think I could. At this time tomorrow, Angie would be Joey Tirenti's. She would be in his bed, his grimy hands touching her body, hurting her and making her do things I only wanted her to do to me.

Sweeping my hand over my face, I leaned forward, staring at the rings in my hand. I'd picked them up when I'd packed, pocketing them. I should have left them there, leaving the memories behind, but I'd been unable. How had things changed so quickly? A woman I hated, one I had despised for years, had suddenly become a craving I couldn't resist until I'd given in and let her overtake everything I was. Letting her change me until she'd unraveled me into pieces I couldn't seem to reform now that I'd lost her. Lost her over an idiotic misunderstanding, something she'd assumed, and, in my anger, I'd validated for her.

The rings danced in my hand as I rolled them around, thinking about the situation. About Angie. One misunderstanding, one wrong decision on my part, and now one day. I sat back, my brows knitting as I thought back to my conversation with Mason. Everything about this seemed wrong. Donelli was caving, but Tirenti was pressuring him. But why so fast? Why tomorrow? Even with as entrenched in security and violence as the families were, they celebrated things like weddings. They were careful, discreet about them, but they were still celebrations. One day didn't allow for guests, for family, for the things that were usually involved.

Tirenti had been suspicious of how quickly Angie and I had gotten married when we'd given him the story. Now he was doing the same thing with Joey, hastening a wedding. There was something there, something going down. My instincts were on edge, screaming at me that I was missing something. Rising, I dropped the rings on the bed where the scarf sat and headed to Mason's room.

Banging on the door, I heard his grumbling as Casey answered. Her cheeks were flush, her curls messy.

"Do you two ever stop?"

She stuck her tongue out and I ignored Mason's comment about using it the right way. He was sitting up in bed with no shirt on, his pants unbuttoned and the bulge below looking uncomfortably hard.

"Keep that erection in check, buddy, or I'll change my mind about letting you have my sister."

Casey reached up and smacked the back of my head.

"That's my girl," Mason said as she hopped back in bed with him.

"You two are gonna kill me."

"Then leave," she said, snuggling into his hold. She looked blissful and, to be honest, I'd never seen her as happy as she was when she was with Mason. Nor had I seen him as happy before Casey.

"Something about tomorrow doesn't feel right," I told them.

"Aside from the fact that the love of your life is about to marry another man?"

"A slimy weasel who disrespects, rapes, and murders women," I growled.

"It's rumor, Ty. We still don't have proof," Mason said, but I could tell from the way he'd unconsciously pulled Casey further into him he believed the rumors as much as I did.

"Still, he's a creep," I groused. "And she's not the love of my life," I added, hearing the mistruth in my words.

"Keep telling yourself that, Ty," Casey said.

"What do you want to do, buddy?" Mason asked.

I knew what I wanted to do. I wanted to stop this, to steal her away from this debacle, and make love to her the way I'd avoided, because that was something I didn't do. Making love was emotional, and I didn't do emotion. Sex for me was raw and dirty, emotionless, without commitment, without attachment. At least it had been until Angie. Now all I desired was to hold her in my arms like Mason was holding Casey.

"I want to go to Armina. I want to get Angie and make her mine."

Casey beamed, her excitement reflected in the way her hazel eyes glittered and how she was nearly jumping out of the bed. I glared at her, not needing her sunny disposition, even if it usually made everything better.

"Then we go. I had the plane fueled up, and the crew is on standby."

"You knew?" I asked, my eyes wide with surprise.

"My best friend doesn't do love," he said with a shrug. "I knew you'd go after her once you pulverized your fists." He pointed to the split skin on my knuckles.

"When do we leave?" I asked, trying not to let my excitement show. I couldn't because as much as I was looking forward to claiming Angie for myself, there were too many unknowns in the way. The risks were high that one of us wouldn't make it out alive or that I would lose her forever. And they were risks I normally would have avoided, but for Angie, I'd face them all.

Chapter Fourteen

ANGIE

The dress lay spread on my bed and as my stylist, Randi, tugged and twisted my hair into form, I couldn't pull my eyes from it. A wedding dress. The idea was appalling. The dress was insulting. The thought of marrying Joey Torenti was terrifying.

I tried not to let the shake in my hands show, instead focusing on finding anything I liked about the dress the asshole had sent over for me. There was no way he hadn't already had it, expecting that I'd marry him the first time his gross hands had tried touching me. That first time, I'd been sixteen, and he'd cornered me. Unlike Tyson, he hadn't cared that I was too young, that he was older than me. His hands had slithered over my skin until my father caught him. The intent had been there, the darkness in his eyes that wasn't the sexy kind Tyson's eyes held. This was evil. From that day forward, my father and Tony had kept me away from him anytime there was a meeting. My father had warned Joey's father, and Joey had turned his interest elsewhere, my father not letting him in our home again until recently when his old friend Rocco Tirenti had decided he had power over my father now that the Bad Omen had infiltrated us and weakened him.

Randi finished my hair and turned to the makeup kit she'd brought. She prepped my face, applying a base layer of concealer. With each pat of her fingers over my freckles, I thought of Tyson and how his eyes softened when he saw them. The way he'd called me beautiful. As much as I wanted to hate him for hurting me, I couldn't close my heart off or stop the leap of it every time I thought of him. He'd fractured my hold on it and now I couldn't seem to piece myself back together.

Stopping Randi, I shook my head. "No makeup, just a light powder. Take the rest off." Confusion reflected in her expression, her mouth pursing. "Just do it."

As she cleaned my face, I tried desperately to think of a way to stop this, but none came. If I ran away, the Tirenti's would turn on my father. But if I stayed... The trembling in my hands grew and I squeezed them together. I needed to be strong for my family, but it was something I'd never been. Tony was the strong one, not me. I was the one who partied and drank and slept with random men. The one who spent money and lived a lavish life supported by my father's crimes. I didn't get involved in any of it. In fact, I pretended I didn't know why we were so rich, why I only left with a security detail, or why people hopped to attention when I entered a store.

Strong wasn't something I was. Everything about me was a façade, one I'd built to make me look strong, to have others fear me the way they did my father, a wall of pride and self-serving confidence that had done nothing but push people away. Everyone but Tyson who had gravitated toward it, matching me in every way. I looked down at my newly manicured nails, tempted to rip them off but deciding I could use them to rip Joey's eyes out when he was forcing himself on me later.

"How's that?" Randi asked, picking up her mirror and showing me. My reflection stared back at me and in it, I saw my mother. Her large brown eyes, her round face, the petite nose with the trace of freckles scattered over it and onto her cheeks.

The beautiful woman I'd loved so desperately that when she'd died, I'd hidden the parts of her that were reflected in me. Rebelling against her because I was angry that she'd died and looking at myself hurt just as it hurt my father and brother.

My fingers brushed over my birthmark lightly, like my mother's had always done.

"Perfect," I said.

Randi relaxed and packed up her things as I moved to my bed, fingering the wedding dress.

"Can you help me put this on?" I asked. There was no one else here to ask. No mother, no sister, no friends. I didn't have friends. No one liked the woman I'd become. Bitter, expectant, rude. The only one who tolerated me was Casey and even she wasn't here.

As Randi helped me pull the gaudy dress on, I could see her thoughts on the changing expression on her face. She wouldn't have made a good poker player.

"It's bad, isn't it?" I asked as she zipped me up.

"It's...different."

I laughed at her attempt not to insult the thing. "It wasn't my choice, so don't hold back on my account."

A full-length mirror sat in the corner of my bedroom, its silver feet always reminding me of alligator feet. I walked to it, trying to contain my gasp. The dress reflected who I'd become over the years, a woman who flaunted her body to tempt men, not caring how much skin I was showing or how little material covered my body. It was not the dress of a little girl's dreams. A man who wanted to flaunt his new trophy had picked this dress. A blatant statement of ownership, one meant to invoke envy in other men, was what this dress stood for. And I didn't want to be owned by Joey Tirenti because another man still owned me, even if he hadn't intended to. Even if none of it had been real.

I turned, looking at the back. It scooped so low, the top of my ass showed, the pink lace of my panties peeking above the edge. I tugged at them, looking at Randi.

"I don't think you're supposed to wear underwear with that kind of dress," she said, her eyes holding the judgement any woman would give the owner of this dress. It was the judgement that typically sat in the eyes of women who gave me side glances filled with jealousy.

"You don't say," I remarked, turning back to see how far down the neckline plunged. Two thin strips of material held my breasts up, leaving the sides of them showing. "This is horrible. I look like I'm going clubbing and not walking down the aisle. Who wears this?"

She stayed silent and with as long as she'd been doing my hair, she was trying not to answer that I would. Because it was the truth. But even I wouldn't have worn this to get married.

With a huff, I sent her away, knowing I had no choice but to suck it up and make it work. The old me would have flaunted it and strutted down the aisle. But I wasn't the old me anymore. Tyson had changed me, and I hadn't even noticed until now.

A knock at the door caught my attention and Tony peeked in. "Hey, Anj—" He stepped into the room, a disapproving look in his eyes. He'd always hated the way I dressed, that big brother in him always coming out. "What the hell are you wearing?"

I picked up the long bottom of the dress, the silk soft in my hands, the slit that sat on my upper thigh moving to reveal my leg and the tiny stilettos below.

"Anj, I can see through that. You are not wearing that out there with all those men."

"It wasn't my pick, Tony. This is what Joey sent for me."

His jaw clenched, the brown of his eyes growing more intense. "I hate that prick. If I could kill him, I would. I hate that dad's selling you off to him to keep the peace, that Torenti is basically blackmailing him, turning on him after all these years. They've been friends since they were young and suddenly he's pressuring pops. I don't like it."

"I know, but we have to deal with it."

He came closer, lifting my face, his eyes lightening. "You look so much like mom." His finger touched my cheek, sweeping over my freckles. "I'd almost forgotten you had her freckles." I stayed quiet as his eyes searched mine. "Anj, what happened with Raines?"

I tried to look away, but he forced my eyes to his.

"I'm in love with him," I admitted, my voice barely a whisper.

"And he did this?" he asked, gesturing to my natural face.

I nodded. "He likes me this way...at least that's what he said."

"Then why did you leave? You were safe with him, Angie. He would have protected you like I want to do."

"Because he doesn't love me. It was all part of the game. And I needed to get away because it hurt too much to stay."

Tony kissed my forehead, pulling me into his arms, and I held onto him, remembering all the times he'd been my rock when we were little and knowing letting me marry Joey Tirenti was killing him as much as it was killing me. But neither of us had a choice. This was our father's decision, a move to bring security to our territory and to the family.

But as Tony left the room, I wondered if that was really the case because something deep inside of me knew no part of this felt right. As if to solidify that notion, Joey barged in a few minutes after Tony left.

"Damn, baby, you look hot." I cringed at the nickname, one I only ever wanted to hear from Tyson, a man who would never say that word to me again.

"I'm not supposed to look hot in a wedding dress, dipshit." I tried to walk around him, but he grabbed my arm, his fingers sinking painfully into my flesh.

"You'll look hot if I want you to. Not that it matters because as soon as you're mine, I plan to rip this thing off and fuck you so hard your father and brother will hear your screams."

I tried to pull away, but he jerked me against him.

"What is this shit?" he asked, rubbing my cheek roughly as if he could rub away my freckles. He gripped my chin so tight it must have bruised. "I don't want damaged goods."

I smacked his arm as his grip grew tighter. "I'm not damaged goods, asshole. They've always been there."

He tried wiping at my birthmark, his thumb digging into my skin and scratching at it.

"Get your hands off me, Joey," I said, fighting to free myself.

He threw me and I landed hard against my vanity, my things falling to the ground with the impact. Rolling his neck, he stalked over to me, grabbed me by my neck, and dragged me across the room. I fought, ripping my nails into his skin, but he overpowered me and slammed me into the wall, knocking the wind from me.

"You are my property, Angie. I didn't know I needed to inspect my property before I took possession of it, but apparently, I do."

"I'm not yours," I rasped, grabbing at his hand. I was struggling to breathe. His hold on my neck was so strong that it took all my effort to remain conscious.

"Oh but you will be. And I've been waiting a long time to get my hands on this body." My stomach twisted violently as his hand dug up the slit of the dress and he yanked at my panties. "No, no. These don't work with this dress, baby." He ripped the delicate material, his hand rubbing between my thighs as he pushed them down.

"Get off me, Joey." This time my words came out so strained they sounded like a gurgle. I kicked my legs at him, but my fight only encouraged him.

"You're going to be so fun to break. I think I'll test you out now." He shoved my underwear down further and I managed to let out a high-pitched scream that sounded more like a squeak.

His touch was vile and my skin crawled. Panic welled in me. No matter how much I fought, this man would own me in a matter of hours, and I knew no amount of fighting him would keep his hands from me.

"Get the fuck off my sister." Tony yanked him from me and threw him across the room.

The breath filled my lungs, and I fell to the floor, trying to gain control of my body, but I was shaking too badly.

"Your sister is mine. I was just making sure my goods aren't damaged."

Tony punched him. "You don't touch her. Understand? You touch and I'll kill you!"

A deep, vicious laugh came from Joey as he pulled himself from the floor. "I'm gonna touch every inch of that body. Touch it, bruise it, lick it. Whatever I want to do to it because I own that body now."

He was in Tony's face, and I could see Tony was trying not to kill him. His fists were clenched so tight, the white strained beneath them.

"She's not yours yet and if you disrespect her, I'll hunt you down and start a territory war if I need to."

"You think you're so bad, don't you, Tony Donelli? Well, maybe if you'd bothered to show any interest in daddy's business besides the booze and drugs it provided, I'd be worried about your threats. But since you didn't, you don't scare me. You're nothing but a bratty little boy, just as bratty as your sister is. And I'm going to enjoy watching you fall while I'm pounding the brains out of her."

He shoved Tony out of the way, grabbed the panties from the floor, and stomped out the door. "If I see another pair of panties under that dress, I'll bend you over and fuck you in front of everyone in that church."

The door slammed, and the tears pushed behind my eyes, threatening to escape. Tony turned his gaze to me, the hurt, the pain, the wound to his pride burning in it. We'd done this to ourselves, neither of us taking our lives seriously, ignoring our father's attempts to train us, to bring us in, and pretending we were in an insulated bubble that no one could pop. But they had, and now we were both precariously teetering on the thin line that remained.

Tony stormed out of the room, and I dropped my head to my hands, wishing I could turn time back and take back my words and actions with Tyson. To return to yesterday and not have gone down that hall, not have said the horrible things I'd said to him, not have fought with him. Not have left. Wishing I could be in his arms, safe and secure, even if he didn't love me. But there was no going back. I had made my choice and now I had to deal with the consequences. My family's survival depended on it.

MY FATHER HAD PULLED strings and booked the church. The priest was close to my family and my father contributed to the church regularly in more than just monetary ways. I didn't understand why we couldn't just do it at the house, but Tirenti had insisted we use the church, saying it wouldn't be right not to. As if Joey were a religious man. There was a special place reserved for his kind when he died.

I nervously clenched the bouquet of roses Tony handed me when he and our men had escorted me to the car. They were from my father's rose garden, his pride and joy aside from me and Tony. I peeked through the church doors as I stood in the vestibule, keeping my sore ankle lifted slightly as I waited for my father. Joey was standing at the front of the church in a tux. If he hadn't been such a scumbag, I would have thought him handsome, but I knew the man below the suit, below the put together façade. He stood proud, his head held high as he looked down the aisle. Tony stood on the other side, scowling at him. Both had their henchmen, hands on their guns, and I noted the tension from where I stood.

There were no bridesmaids, no pretty flowers to line the pews, no guests but the handful Tirenti had brought and he'd given my father time to invite. This wasn't the dream wedding I'd always envisioned with the white carriage, the princess dress, the tiara I'd always wanted. No ring bearer or flower girl to drop rose petals down the aisle. Not even an organist. I wanted to cry, to run and stop this. My father's hand on my shoulder calmed the panic.

"The jackass is taking you to his house as soon as the wedding is over," he grumbled.

I looked up at him, seeing the sadness in his eyes. He turned me to him, his eyes lighting as he brushed his thumb softly over my cheek.

"I missed these," he said. "You look so much like your mother, sweetheart."

I turned my eyes down, saying, "I thought that made you sad."

He tilted my chin up. "Never. Seeing how you hid them as if you didn't want to remember her made me sad."

The pressure behind my eyes built, and I struggled to keep my tears hidden from him.

"Your mother was beautiful, and you have her beauty." He touched my birthmark, leaning in and giving it a gentle kiss. "And this, the mark of the gods, your mother used to call it."

I laughed through the tears that slipped free.

"She loved how special you were. She loved you both very much and this would hurt her. I'm glad she's not here to see what's become of me. Selling you off to Tirenti, knowing what he's like."

He tipped my chin, tracing the tenderness that Joey's grip had left on my neck. His eyes grew a shade darker. "Did he do this? Or did Raines?"

I shook my head. "No, it wasn't Tyson. He never hurt me physically." But I couldn't say he hadn't hurt me emotionally.

"Joey?" The word came out tersely, his teeth gritted.

"I'm fine, Daddy. Let's get this over with."

"I'm sorry, Angela." I could see the tears welling behind his eyes and I took his hand, pushing my shoulders back and holding my head high.

"Nothing to be sorry about. It's a business arrangement. Just like what you had with Tyson. It's for the family, for our legacy. Now walk me down the aisle in this sorry excuse for a wedding gown while I pretend I'm dressed in high fashion."

His smile made what waited for me easier to bear, and he took my arm in his, nodding to our men to open the doors. Three of our men led the way, not bridesmaids in lovely dresses, not a maid of honor to lift the long train I wished followed me. When my father reached Joey, there was a tense moment when I thought he would back out or pull his gun and shoot him. Joey took my hand, my skin crawling at his touch, and jerked it from my father.

"You hurt her, and I don't care what kind of deal I have with your father," my father muttered low enough for only Joey to hear before he kissed my head and walked away, his head held high.

I couldn't help that sense that something was going to happen. My father was emotional, but still too calm. He was marrying his only daughter off to a scumbag who treated women like shit, and he was making some kind of deal with Tirenti to keep him appeased and off his back. Not to mention there was no sign of Mason. Three bosses may have ruled this province, but they all deferred to Mason, even Tirenti. But Mason had left before I arrived. It may have had to do with Tyson and what had happened between us, but that still didn't explain the strange foreboding sensation I had.

Joey jerked me against him and licked my ear.

"Get the fuck off her! You're not married yet," Tony said,

moving toward me. The tension grew like a heavy fog that sat ready to envelop us all.

"She'll be mine in a matter of minutes," he said. Then, lowering his mouth to my ear, he said, "And I plan to use every inch of that body. My cuffs and rope are ready."

My heart thudded in fear, but I pushed him away. "You wouldn't know how to handle someone like me, Joey. I've been telling you that for years."

"Well, let's not wait any longer to test that out, baby." Again with that word that sent bile burning my throat each time he said it. That was Tyson's nickname for me, that and viper, and the thought of Joey taking ownership of a word that had once made my legs squeeze was almost enough to make me vomit. "Get on with it, priest," he snapped, pulling his tux back to show the butt of his gun.

He glanced back at me. "I'm gonna put that to use later, too. See how you look coming around it."

A strangled cry slipped through my mouth because as adventurous as I was, weapon play had never been my thing. I was risky, but only to a point, and that was my stopping point.

"That gun goes anywhere near my sister's body, and I'll shoot your cock off," Tony growled.

I didn't turn to him, knowing he was desperately trying to find a way out of this, just like I was.

"Let's go," Joey said to the priest.

The ceremony began, but I didn't listen to the words. My mind was going through everything I'd done wrong in the past twenty-four hours. My eyes glanced at the back of the church, hoping to see Tyson burst through and save me, but that was fantasy. He hated me and he was probably still at the resort, having sex with the manager in my place and pretending he never made his mark on me. A mark that would remain no matter how much I tried to remove it and no matter how Joey would try to beat it from me.

The flight to Armina was the second longest I'd ever experienced, the one when we'd gone to save Casey was the first. I paced the cabin while Mason tried to take my mind from Angie. His attempts lacked effort, and I knew his mind was on what awaited us when we got there. This was big. We were going into Donelli's territory unannounced, stopping a wedding between two other families, and likely pissing at least one of them off. There was bound to be gunfire, and someone would be dead by the end of the day. My intention was for that death to be Joey Tirenti's, but there were no guarantees.

"You sure about this, Ty?" Mason asked as the car drew closer to the church listed in the invitation.

"Of course not, but I need to stop this. Even if she hates me forever, there's no way I'm letting Joey Tirenti touch her. I can't believe her brother isn't stopping this."

"He doesn't have a choice. It's Donelli's call, and he's still in charge until he fully hands things over to Tony."

I spotted the church in the distance, my eye picking up movement on the corner of the building. Leaning forward, I put my hand on Breck's shoulder. "Slow down," I said. "Do you see what I see, Mace?"

He leaned forward, picking up his phone. "Turn down the street before the church and park out of sight. Tell Finch to do the same."

We'd come prepared, bringing enough bodies to fight the war we expected.

"Breck, drive by, don't slow down," he said. "Ty, tell me if there's another one posted on the other side. Check the shadows."

I turned my head just enough to see the slight movement of a body in the alley next to the church. "Yeah, at least one."

"That makes two in the front of the church and one at each corner. I'm guessing they have two in the back."

He lifted his phone and sent a text as I eyed him.

"You spotted one on the corner?" I said.

"Yeah. Breck, pull up two blocks down. I don't want any chance of us being seen. And keep your eyes peeled."

I stared at him, waiting for an explanation because if he spotted another man, he was looking before we were close enough.

"I may have suspected Tirenti was going to turn this into a bloodbath."

"Those don't look like his imbeciles," I said, scratching my head. "He's not smooth enough for that. Those are Omens."

"Yeah. After we talked last night, I called Donelli." He pulled his gun out as Breck parked the car. "I told him plans had changed, and I'd text him if our suspicions were true."

"Plans had changed?"

He gave me a haughty grin. "I may have planted the seed that Angie's haste to leave you offered us an opportunity."

My mouth dropped. Leave it to Mason to have a master plan. "Wait, you let him give Angie to Joey?"

"I encouraged him, knowing Tirenti would use it to get what he wants. His son gets Angie, he gets Donelli and the territory.

The Omen get a weasel to control, a weak boss they can manipulate to take down the province. Giving me the prime opportunity to rid myself of a threat."

"Asshole. When we get through this, it's you and me in the boxing ring and I'm gonna mess up that pretty face of yours. Don't ever use my girl as a pawn again," I said, slipping from the car.

We moved to the shadows of the alleys, skirting the buildings until we were close enough. I was coming to realize the Bad Omen were arrogant sons of bitches who thought they were invincible but were making lethal mistakes. They hadn't anticipated me coming for Angie, or Mason wanting Tirenti's head for turning on him. And they were too easy to spot.

"I didn't use your girl. And since when did you start calling her your girl?" he muttered.

"I don't know, but I like it."

"What's the plan, guys?" Breck asked.

"Yeah, we're running out of time," I noted, trying not to think of Angie in there taking vows with Joey.

"Tell Finch to take out the two in the back of the church and scout for any others. Stay silent, break their necks if necessary, but tell them not to make a scene." He gestured for Breck to come closer. "Send Creek up to take the guy on the corner out. You take the one closest to us and let me and Tyson handle the other two. Silencers on, I don't want the men in the church knowing anything is going on out here. I'm sure they have more inside."

"Sounds like a plan." Beck made the call, and I scanned the area, seeing the shadow of the one hidden from view. The other two were in plain sight, but acting like they were undercover, one was reading the paper, the other playing on his phone. Both had their hands on their guns, ready to kill if anything went down.

I spotted Creek, and Mason gave the motion for the three of us to go. Just as Creek shot his man, Breck grabbed his and put him in a neck hold. The one in the alley stepped out and my shot took him down at the same time Mason landed a shot in the neck of the other. Both men stumbled, reaching for their guns, but the second bullet did the job.

"Does this seem too easy to you?" I asked Mason as we took the weapons from the bodies and moved closer.

"Entirely. Either they're hiding more in the church, letting us think this is easy, or they're off their game."

"Again," I noted.

It surprised me that each time we'd had a run in with the Omens, they weren't up to their reputation. They went down too easily, and that didn't seem right. The Omen were like ghosts you didn't see until you were taking your last breath. They didn't stand on corners trying to blend in. They were in the shadows, ready to pounce.

Mason had mentioned the same thing. Either they were getting sloppy, or every move so far had been a way to boost our confidence and ensure we grew complacent. I had suspected the latter was the case and when they chose to really strike, it would be lethal, but now I wasn't so sure. This situation was one that warranted that deadly reputation they'd earned, yet we'd taken every one of their men out with ease.

"How are we doing this?" I asked Mason as we approached the door to the church, still staying low on the side of the building.

"I've got us covered. Donelli's men are standing guard. Tirenti would have agreed, thinking the Omens would take them out first. We're going to surprise Tirenti and walk right in."

"Shit, how did you get this devious?" I asked. Mason amazed me every day with how good he was at this stuff. I was good with my fists, but his brain was his power.

"It's not devious, it's strategic. Ready to win back your girl?"

"Ready as I'll ever be."

"You'll go down the aisle and get her. The rest of the team will take the back and side entrances."

I should have known he had it all planned. Here I'd been thinking this was a risky venture and Mason already had everyone in place to strike. There was still risk. I'd be walking in alone. A target that Tirenti or Joey could easily take out. A distraction while Mason, our men, and Donelli's set the trap.

We walked into the church vestibule. Donelli's men were on guard and gave us an understanding nod. I rolled my neck and shoved the sleeves of my shirt higher to show my muscle then walked into the main part of the church, leaving Mason behind. I kept my steps steady, my shoulders back, even though I knew I was vulnerable, that any of them could take me out.

Angie turned toward me, her brown eyes growing large. She looked stunning, her hair done up in curls that were piled on her head, her veil pinned within them. The dress she wore left little to the imagination, and I tried not to question why I could see right through it and that she clearly had no underwear on. Maybe I'd been wrong, and risking my life like this for her was a tragic mistake.

"Get your hands off my wife!" My voice resounded through the church, cutting through the sound of Tirenti's men raising their guns.

From the corner of my eye, I saw movement in the rafters, but I kept my eyes ahead. If it was Mason or any of our men, one flick of my eyes to their location would give them away. If it was Omen, I was dead.

"What's the meaning of this, Raines?" Joey snarled.

"You're touching my wife, and I can guarantee she doesn't like that touch, not as much as she likes mine."

Tirenti drew his gun, and he moved to the aisle. I was confident he wouldn't shoot and risk Mason's wrath, not without the Bad Omen backing him up. "Go home, Raines, before I fill you with holes. We annulled your marriage. You have no claim here, and she doesn't want you."

I continued forward, wondering where Mason and the others

were. No gunshots had penetrated the uncomfortable silence that hung in the air after Tirenti's threat. That told me either our men had discovered no Omen or had, once again, dispatched of them too easily. The latter I'd contemplate with Mason when this was over.

My instincts were on edge until I spotted Tony pulling his gun out slow enough to go unnoticed by everyone else because their eyes were on me. He was ready for a fight, just like Mason had said. I was still a walking target, so I stopped midway through the building.

"Why don't you let her tell me that," I told Tirenti. "Angela, get over here and tell me I have no claim on you. Tell me how you don't want me."

She moved, and Joey grabbed her arms. That's when I noticed the bruising around her neck. My fists clenched, my anger rising. I couldn't kill him now. She was too close to him and half the people in the room had their guns on me.

"Let me go, Joey."

"I'm not a fool, baby."

I saw the way she cringed at the nickname I'd grown fond of calling her and it made my desire to fill Joey with holes even greater.

"She's not your baby, she's mine," I snapped. "Isn't that right, little viper?"

Her inhale was noticeable, but she played it off. "Let me talk to him. I'll get rid of him and then we can finish here."

He jerked her forward. "You're lying," he snarled.

"Of course, I'm not. I don't want him. I thought I did, and he tossed me aside like a used piece of luggage."

I could hear the truth in her statement, how she'd convinced herself that's what I'd done.

"If he wants me to tell him to his face, then let me. I hate him. I always have. No one hurts Angela Donelli and expects that I'll take him back." She freed her arm, her head going up proudly as she turned to me. I could see the fire in her eyes, the resignation that she wasn't going to break again. In her mind, I'd hurt her and thrown her away, just like she'd said.

Joey pulled his gun out and trained it on me.

"Put the gun down, Joey, and let them talk," Tony said. "It's the least you can do before you take her."

Joey looked at his father, who was hard to read. His muscles were tense, the vein in his neck protruding. All the while, Angie grew closer to me and the closer she came, the more lost in her I became.

"You've got a lot of nerve showing up here, Raines," she said, trying to sound tough. But I could hear the shake in her voice, see the fear in her eyes. She needed me to say the right thing because she wanted me to save her. That confirmation drove me to step closer to her.

"Watch it, Raines. You step any closer to my bride and I'll kill you."

The grinding of my teeth caused my jaw to ache.

"What do you want, Tyson?" Angie asked, her voice low.

"To tell you what you didn't give me a chance to tell you yesterday," I started.

"A chance? You threw me out!"

Damn, I had and of course she would call me out on it.

"Well, you were being a bitch."

"Because you were an ass, a hurtful ass." And there it was, the quiver in her voice that confirmed my suspicion.

I grabbed her arms, pulling her closer.

"That's it," Joey growled, but the sound of more guns being pulled out stopped his complaints. This place was about to erupt, and Angie and I were right in the middle of it.

"I was hurtful because you were. Fuck, Angie, you didn't hear the entire conversation."

"I heard enough!"

The sigh that came from me was one that poured from the

depths of my soul. "No, you didn't, or you'd know that I love you, Angela Donelli." Her mouth parted, the fight leaving her body. "I love you so much that it hurts. You destroyed me, Anj, and nothing can piece me back together but you."

Her bottom lip trembled, and I waited for her response, hearing Joey's growing agitation. My eyes moved to him.

"You can't have her back, Raines! She's mine now."

"Shut up, Joey. She's not yours." I tipped her chin up, seeing the bruising that was forming around her neck. My blood boiled. "And there's no way I'm letting you put your grimy paws on my girl."

"She's mine!" I looked past her, seeing him aim his gun and registering the click of the trigger. I pushed Angie to the ground and his bullet hit me square in the chest, ripping the air from my lungs. I heard Angie scream but my body was crashing to the ground. Gunshots filled the room as the war erupted around us.

"Tyson!" Angie's voice was distant, the pressure of her hands on me too light to do more than drift into my awareness. "Please don't die! Please. I love you. I've always loved you and…"

The words faded just as everything became black and no matter how I tried to fight, to hold on to those words, they were just out of reach, like they'd always been.

Chapter Sixteen

ANGIE

Tyson was there telling me he loved me, and my heart could barely contain the joy that burst through it, but then that joy turned to agony. I laid on his chest, the blood soaking through my white dress. It wouldn't stop, just as my tears wouldn't. The church was a cacophony of gunshots and yelling and I covered my ears, Tyson's blood coating my hair with the move. He wasn't responding, he wasn't moving, and I felt like that bullet had torn through me. It hurt too much to think he might not live. So I laid there with him, my body over his as if I could protect him.

Silence filled the air then the sound of feet running toward me. I braced myself for Joey's hands to rip me from Tyson's body, for the sight of my father and Tony dead. Braced myself for a life of pain, knowing that I had caused this, that if I'd stayed with Tyson, that if I hadn't been so quick to assume, I'd be safe in his arms on the island.

Hands grasped my arms, and I fought, screaming and clawing to stay with him because I couldn't leave him.

"Angie, stop," Tony's voice cut through my desperation, and I stopped struggling and let him pull me to him. "Are you hurt?" he asked, looking me over. He had blood dripping from his arm and his ear where a bullet had nicked it, but otherwise, he looked whole and intact.

I shook my head, unable to form the words.

"Fuck, Ty," I heard Mason say. "Grab him. He's hurt bad." I turned my head to see him and his men picking Tyson up. I hadn't realized he was there, that any of them were there.

"Get him in the car. I'll handle this mess." My father's voice was firm and assured, not the weak man he'd been when he'd walked me into the church. I gripped Tony's shirt, relief filling me that they were both alive.

Mason's men had Tyson, and they were rushing him out. I tried moving to follow, but Tony kept me close.

"Let me go. I need to be with him. Please, Tony."

"No, Angie. Let them take him. Mason's got him, and he won't let anything happen to him."

I turned into his chest. The tears I'd been swallowing back since the moment I'd walked out on Tyson broke free. My body shook with the power of them as Tony held me close in his protective embrace.

"He'll be okay, Anj. Dad's calling the hospital now to make sure he gets the best care. We need to leave before the police get here."

I nodded, but I still couldn't move. Tony scooped me into his arms. He held me the entire trip home, just as he had when we were children, and I would crawl into his bed after our mother died. He would hold me, letting me shed the tears that I hid from others.

When the car pulled up to the house, he helped me out, wiping my tears away and kissing my head.

"I wasn't about to let that slimebag touch you, Anj. Neither was Dad."

I searched his eyes. "But that's what you were doing," I said, trying to understand.

"That's what we wanted Joey to think, for Tirenti to think."

My mouth fell as understanding came to me. "You tricked them? Wait, you used me to trick them?" I punched his arm.

"It was necessary. I didn't know Tyson would come, but I knew Mason would. He and Dad talked before you came home and then again last night. They suspected this was a trap, that Tirenti would turn on us. And he was right. There were Bad Omen outside and hidden inside the church, waiting for Tirenti's signal."

My breath stuck in my throat. Bad Omen again. The last time they'd struck, I'd almost lost Tony. And now, I might lose Tyson.

"Take me to the hospital," I said. "I don't care about all this nonsense, just take me there. I want to see him."

Tony's expression softened. "Anj, he might not make it."

My cry was a heartbroken one that scraped its way through my soul before escaping. I shook my head. "You said he'd make it."

"That gunshot hit him right in the chest."

"You survived."

"I know, but none of the bullets hit anything critical."

And this one had hit Tyson in the chest, close to his heart. I wobbled and Tony caught me.

"Take me to the hospital," I said.

He searched my eyes, looking for some chance that I wasn't serious, but I crossed my arms and stared him down.

"Okay, but wash the blood off you and change. That dress needs to be burned. I'm not taking you anywhere in that thing. Then I'll take you."

My normal smart assed retorts were out of reach so I pulled his head down and gave him a kiss on the cheek. The trip to my room seemed endless, the pain in my ankle a minor irritation from what sat in my chest. So much had transpired over the past few days. My life had changed. I had changed. Tyson was the reason and now I stood to lose him. I pushed the thought aside, knowing it would leave me frozen if I let it linger.

When I reached my bathroom, I washed the blood from my face and body, hating how much layered my skin and that I was washing what could be the last touch of Tyson from me. I threw the dress in the trash, never wanting to see it again. My hands were shaking as I dug through my closet for something to wear, thinking of Tyson's comment to me before my life had fallen apart. That I needed to change my revealing outfit. I'd always worn revealing clothes, flaunting my body to gain the attention of men. Leaving nothing to the imagination. But that didn't seem right now. Tyson loved me. The words had burned through me, carving their place in my heart and my soul. I was his, and I didn't need other men to look at me, to touch me. Because I had his touch.

My knees buckled, and I caught myself, reality hitting me that he was dying and might not make it to touch me again. That the last touch of his hands on my arms as he told me he loved me might have been the last. I choked back the sob that was dragging its way through my body. Digging in the back of my closet, an urgency pounding through me, I grabbed a T-shirt and shorts, something I never would have worn and wasn't even sure how they were in my closet. I slipped on a pair of sandals and, knowing the hospital would be cold, snagged a sweater I'd kept that had been my mother's. It was a soft pink cardigan that hung loose on me, just as it had on her. I could almost smell her perfume on it and the thought comforted me.

With a deep breath, I tore through the house, finding Tony waiting for me in the foyer. He wore a fresh shirt, and had a bandage on his ear.

"Ready?" he asked, eyeing my outfit.

"No," I answered honestly.

"He's in surgery. I just got off the phone with Mason."

That sob pushed to free itself again, but I shoved it away. I had to be strong because Tyson couldn't be, and my strength couldn't waiver or I might lose him. And that would leave me too broken to ever return.

RAIN POUNDED ON THE WINDOW, the storm beyond raging like my emotions had raged for days. Tyson had made it through surgery, but he'd been unconscious for days. The bullet had just missed his heart and the thought that mere centimeters had meant the difference between life and death still caused tears to surface. Casey and Mason kept watch with me, taking shifts, but I hadn't left the room, afraid he'd wake or worse while I was away. Tony sat with me sometimes, bringing me food and clean clothes. Every day that passed was another where I replayed the events over and over in my mind, a constant punishment for having made the decisions that had led us to this point.

I looked out at the rain, pressing my face to the cool window and twisting the rings Tyson had given me around my finger. Pulling the cardigan closer to me, the silk of the scarf I'd snuggled with the night I'd stayed in his bed caressed my cheek. Casey had found it when she cleaned out the bag with his clothes. He'd had it in his pocket along with the rings and I hadn't been able to give either of them up, both reminding me of what we'd had, what I'd almost lost, what I still could lose.

"You know, little viper, when you said you wanted to kill me all those times, I didn't think you really meant it." My heart leaped, and I turned to find Tyson's weary eyes watching me.

I couldn't contain my smile, especially when he gave me that sexy smirk that made my insides weak.

"Well, if I'd known you'd be such an easy target, I would have attempted it years ago," I replied, hesitant to go to him, afraid that what had happened between us would erase the words he'd confessed at the church. The pain of him throwing me aside and taking the bullet for me was still present. The guilt that it should have been me, that I'd caused all of this, that he wouldn't have been hurt if I'd just stayed with him, if I wasn't so stubborn.

I fidgeted with the rings. His eyes dropped to them, his expression falling. He looked so pale, the powerful man I loved weak because of me.

"You went through with it?" His voice held a sadness that seemed juxtaposed with the man I knew.

I glanced down at the rings, understanding dawning on me. Rising, I moved closer, still fearful of getting too close, of believing he still loved me, of believing he could forgive me for leaving him and getting him shot.

"No, Joey's dead. Tony took him down when he shot you."

"Is that what hurts so bad?"

I nodded, swallowing. "I'm sorry, Tyson." My voice was so low it was barely a murmur. "I'm sorry I left you. I'm sorry I caused this, that you got hurt because of me."

He reached out and grabbed my hand, his fingers sliding over the rings. "Are these mine?"

I met his eyes, seeing the hope there. His ring had been on his finger when he'd come to rescue me and I rubbed my finger over it, seeing how his eyes lit. "Of course, stupid," I said, trying to return to the woman I'd been before this experience had transformed me. To return to what made us whole. "Unless you were talking about another wife when you busted into that church."

He yanked me to him, cringing as I lost my balance and crashed into him.

"Tyson, I'm sorry," I said, trying to stand, worried that I'd damaged him. He threaded his fingers into my hair and pulled me to him, his kiss so full of emotion, I couldn't help but lose myself in it. My body relaxed, the worry that had built, the fear of everything that had happened all fading as my chest warmed.

"You seriously need a breath mint," I muttered, causing him to laugh.

"That's my girl." He let me go, his fingers capturing the scarf and skimming it as I backed from his embrace.

"Casey gave it to me. It was in your pocket with my rings. Is that okay?"

"Your rings?" he asked, his brow raising.

"My rings, my husband, the man I love and have loved since the moment I saw him standing in the foyer of our home proud and sexy, even with his tattoos, old age, and rude comments."

"I'm not an old man, baby. I'm experienced. Experienced enough to make you come undone like you never have. Now get your sexy ass in this bed and let me touch that body."

"You just woke up! You have stitches, your wound—"

"I don't give a shit, wife. Get your ass over here and let me touch you."

I curled into the bed next to him, trying not to disturb all the tubes and monitors that were hooked up to him.

"What are you wearing?" he asked, kissing my nose as I looked up at him. "I don't think I've ever seen you in so much clothing. Where's all your skin?"

"You said you wanted me covered up so no other man could see what's yours," I said, noting the strength that still sat in his chest and being careful not to disturb his wound.

"So I did. Now, tell me what happened after that asshole shot me, why my best friend isn't here and my sister... Shit, is he fucking her when I'm in here with all this shit attached to me?"

Laughing, I said, "No, although I'm not sure they haven't. They take shifts but Casey left to get showered and changed. Mason is meeting with my father, Tony, and Strint to figure out what to do with Tirenti's territory. Now that they've toppled his family, his hold on the territory has left it open for the Omens. They're working out a plan to either split the territory between us and Strint or hand it over to someone else."

"Huh, likely Rinagi. He was part of Tirenti's crew, but Tirenti pissed him off a year back and he's been building his own empire on the outskirts of the territory. He's young, and he's smart. And Mason has him in our pockets already. Makes sense to move him into power."

"Rinagi? That name sounds familiar. I think I hooked up with someone by that name a while back," I teased. His arm squeezed tight around me, his heartbeat monitor pinging loudly.

"Do I need to kill someone when I get out of this place?"

"I think you'd have too many to kill, just like I think I would. And I'm just playing. I don't know him." I kissed his cheek. "I'm all yours, Tyson. Body, heart, and soul."

He peered down at me, the amber in his eyes sparkling. "You love me, Anj?" he asked, his voice a soft whisper that tingled along my ears.

"Yes, completely. Do you really love me?"

He was quiet for a moment. "Is that scar big?"

I scrunched my brows. "What?"

"The scar from that bullet I took for you. Is it big?"

I nodded, not sure what that had to do with loving me.

"Good, I think I'll get a new tattoo to cover it. A long black viper." My breath caught, my chest growing tight. "And you can get a matching one, someplace that marks you as mine, Angela Donelli, because I'm not letting you go again. No matter how much you fight me or how loud you complain. I'll smack that ass red if I have to, but I'm never letting you go."

Bringing his face close, I held his cheek, gazing into his eyes. "Then I expect you to make this marriage real, Tyson Raines. I want a pretty dress, lots of flowers, and horses."

"Horses? What the hell do horses have to do with a wedding?"

"We can't have it on the beach like I really want, so we'll have to have it on your stinky horse farm."

He stopped my words with a kiss, pulling me into him even though I knew it was hurting him. "My girl wants a beach wedding, my girl gets a beach wedding. My girl gets whatever she wants, and I'll kill anyone who stands in the way of me giving it to her."

"I love you Tyson, and all I want is you."

"Good, because there's no way I'm ever letting another man touch this body again. It's mine. You belong to me, little viper."

He kissed me again, his hand sliding along my body.

"If you bust yourself up again, I'll kill you myself," I heard Mason say.

Tyson nibbled my lip and let me go, his eyes twinkling with humor. "If it's anybody that's going to take me out, it's this one, Mace."

"Damn right it is," I said. I brushed my fingers over the growth that lined his face.

"You like that, baby?"

"It's sexy."

"All right, you two. Don't make me call a nurse in here and have Angie removed from the hospital."

Tyson smacked my ass, and I took the hint, climbing from him.

"Damn, you got me hard, Anj. I don't see why you can't take care of that after Mason leaves."

Mason put his hand on his hips, shaking his head. "Heal, and then she can blow you all you want. Until then, off limits."

I pouted my lip, causing Tyson to comment on how that wasn't helping.

"Can you give us a few, Angie?" Mason asked, taking a seat across from the bed.

"Of course."

Tyson gestured me over with his finger and I kissed him again, his fingers gripping my hair so hard it soaked me. Getting him to take it slow and heal was going to be a challenge. When he let me go, I was breathless, and he was beaming. His smile lit every part of me that his kiss hadn't reached, and as I left the room, I knew everything was going to work out. Tyson was mine, and I was his. All the animosity between us had shadowed the desire, hiding what we truly were, two people who needed each other, and who loved each other desperately. And Tyson loved me—freckles, birthmark, glasses, spoiled attitude, and snarky remarks. He loved everything about me and that made me complete for the first time in far too long, and I knew I would spend the rest of my life letting him see those parts of me I'd hidden and letting him love them.

Angie was spread out on a beach towel, her tan skin a glorious honey tone, her knee propped up so that my eyes followed the curve to where the string of her pink bikini rested on her luscious hip. Just looking at her had me hard. I licked my lips, eager to slip my tongue up her skin and taste the sweat that had beaded on her toned stomach.

"You ever drag me out to a place like this again and I'll make sure that bullet hits the target next time, Raines," Greyson Tides groused as he moved beside me.

"I don't think I'm the one who dragged you here. That would be your fiancé, Tides."

"A beach? Couldn't you have it someplace normal?"

I glanced over at him, unhappy that I had to draw my eyes from Angie's body. "Normal?" He looked uncomfortable in his white button down and black slacks. "Do you ever relax, Tides?"

"Never. Relaxing is for pussies like you and Brinks."

"Damn, remind me why I had to invite you again?"

He tore his eyes from Riley, giving me a wicked grin. "Because we're business associates now and baby girl would have cut me off from that sexy body for a painful amount of time if I'd kept her from it."

My jaw ticked. "Don't let Mason hear you say that and don't call her baby girl. It's as bad as Mason calling Casey princess. Makes me want to punch you both."

"I'd like to see you try it." He swallowed his shot of bourbon and set the glass down on the bar with a loud thump.

"I think that staff member's getting a little flirty with my sister, Tides," Mason said, approaching us. He gestured toward where Riley and Casey were standing in the shallow water, giggling. Both had bikinis on that covered more skin than Angie's, but not enough. I hated the way my sister dressed and since I considered Riley to be another sister, I hated seeing her out of her normal conservative clothes.

"Isn't that bikini a little skimpy for Riley, Tides? I'd want to cover her up so that guy can't see all that skin," I said, trying to irritate him, but irritating myself instead.

"Says the man whose bride has almost every inch exposed." He adjusted his sleeves and ignored my glare. "Guess I need to go show that boy it's not nice to mess with another man's woman. And I'll need to remind Riley there are consequences to showing what's mine to other men."

I stared at him as he walked away with the confident swagger of a man who shouldn't be messed with.

"Does it piss you off when he talks like that, Mace? 'Cause it sure pisses me off." I glanced at him, holding back my laugh. His jaw was so tight I was waiting to hear it pop. "I'll take that as a yes."

"Fucker," he muttered, grabbing a drink the bartender had set out. The two I'd ordered for me and Angie were waiting for me to take them, but I let them be.

"He's good for her. As much as it frustrates the two of us." When I turned back, Tides had Riley thrown over his shoulder and was storming from the beach, a playful smirk on his face.

Riley was giggling, and I didn't want to imagine what was going to happen in that hotel room for the rest of the day.

"That's good for her?" Mason asked.

"As good as you are for Casey. If I have to hear you making her squeal in the kitchen, you can watch Tides own your sister."

Casey was making her way over to us.

"Why are you wearing that skimpy thing, Case?" I asked, as Mason grabbed her and pulled her in for a kiss.

"Because my man likes it, that's why," she said, pushing from his arms with a laugh.

"Damn right I do. Sexiest thing here," he said, smacking her ass and making her jump.

"Don't make me hurt you," I warned him.

Casey kissed me on the cheek. "Settle down, big brother. You've got your hands full with Angie. Stop worrying about me."

"I never stop worrying about you."

Mason folded his arms around her and pulled her back against his chest. "I worry about her now," he said, nibbling on her neck.

She leaned her head back on him. "How long are we staying?" she asked.

"Till the morning. Tides is flying out with Riley at dawn. We leave a few hours later. Why? Do you have plans for us, princess?"

I rolled my eyes. "I don't want to hear them, whatever they are." I grabbed the drinks from the bar. "I'm going to torment my wife. You two keep the hands to yourself or take it to your room like Tides did. And if you don't, I'll tell you everything he's likely doing to your sister until I aggravate you enough that you leave."

"Asshole," Mason grumbled as I walked away.

"You love me, buddy."

"Is that what they call it?"

Shaking my head, I made my way to Angie. My wife. It seemed surreal to say, but we'd married earlier in the day with the morning sun shining down on her hair, highlighting the strawberry strands that were growing in. I'd promised her a beach wedding, and I'd delivered, booking the resort and ensuring we had it to ourselves by canceling everyone who'd booked for the weekend. There'd been some bruised egos, but I'd made up for it by throwing in some amenities. Their complaints had been worth it when she'd walked down the aisle toward me.

Joey had ruined her dream wedding, so I gave her something even better. With pink rose petals and white sand as her aisle, she had looked like a goddess in her white dress. Not see-through and skin flaunting but stylish and stunning. She'd beamed at me when she'd handed her bouquet of pink and white flowers to Casey right before her father placed her hands in mine.

Pink. Of course the flowers were pink, just like the material that had draped the archway where we stood and the dresses Riley and Casey had worn. Because if my girl wanted pink for our wedding colors, she was getting it.

I'd been the last person anyone had imagined getting married and here I'd gone and done it before everyone else. Tides and Riley were planning to tie the knot in another month, pushing their intended early April wedding back while I healed and made my marriage to Angie official. Tides hadn't been happy that his plans with Riley had been moved again but Riley, who was as obnoxious as Casey about me getting married, had worked her magic on him and let me sneak in first. Something I'd taken great pleasure in reminding him of all day.

Mason and Casey hadn't set a date for their wedding yet, wanting to enjoy the freshness of their relationship before they took the step, but he had bought her a massive diamond ring that now sat on her finger, one that Angie instantly compared to her own. I'd had to buy her a second ring to wrap over it just to satisfy her.

My girl was spoiled, and I didn't care. I intended to continue spoiling her for the rest of my life.

"You know, if you keep that leg at that angle, it's gonna tempt me to slide between them and take you right here, Anj." I set the drinks down as she lifted to her elbows and peered up at me, the sun shining in her eyes and turning them golden. "That doesn't help. Now you're just teasing me."

She licked her lips, and I groaned, dropping next to her and pulling her onto my lap. "When are you not ready to fuck me, Raines?" she asked, sitting up on my erection, which lurched at the move.

"I'm always ready to fuck you, Mrs. Raines." I cupped her breast, her nipple prominent through the thin material of her suit.

"You wanna take your hands off my sister, Raines?" Tony called from across the beach.

"That would be a no, Tony. Don't you have a territory to run? I'd suggest you stop acting like you're on vacation, get out of your swim trunks and on a plane home, and mind your damn business."

"I'm always dressed like this, Raines," he said before turning back to flirting with the girl serving drinks.

"Are you going to yell at him for flirting with my staff, or do I have to do that?" I asked Angie as her hand rubbed over the black viper that coiled around my scar, fangs bared. The damned wound hadn't healed enough when I got inked so I decided to keep the scar prominent as evidence of what I'd do to protect my girl and make the tattoo evidence of what I'd do to my enemies if they ever touched her again.

"Why don't you forget about him and tell me how much you love me," she said, dropping on me. I moved my hands to her ass, squeezing the firm skin and pushing her into my dick.

"Yeah, I think we need to take this someplace more private, baby. I really want you right now."

"Dirty old man," she teased before slipping from my hold. She lifted herself and my eyes followed the move of her body, the way her tits bounced when she stood. "I'm going upstairs to take this suit off. I have a toy that can give me attention if you don't want to play."

I scrambled up, following her. "No way that toy is taking the place of my cock. Now, if you want to play with that some before I have my turn, I'm down with watching that."

She turned, walking backward, and gave me a devious smile. "Why don't you help me with it and if you really want, you can join it."

"Damn, that sound like a plan." I smacked her ass hard, the sound loud enough for Tony to yell at me. Snatching her up into my arms, I carried her back to the building, her arms encircling my neck as I took us to our honeymoon suite, plans of ravaging her the rest of the night and into the next day possessing my mind. But as I threw her on the bed, crawling over her, those big brown eyes looked up at me with nothing but love and all plans to take her hard like I always did disappeared. Instead, I made love to her, relishing in the experience of connecting with her on a level that only existed for Angie, one that had always been hers to own and to claim and forever would be.

Thank you for reading Hostile Cravings. Be sure to look for **Unhinged Cravings**, the final chapter in the Cravings world, coming soon.

Emerson Tides is ready to face his brother but when a slip-up puts Ava in his hands, his plans quickly derail.

If you enjoyed Tyson and Angie's story, please consider leaving a review. Reviews are like priceless gems authors cherish.

About the Author

J. L. Jackola is a writer of love stories with fantasy, darkness, feisty women, and morally gray men. She's an admitted sugar addict with a penchant for anything with salted caramel. When she's not weaving tales, snacking on sweets, or downing her morning cup of tea, you can find her logging miles in her running shoes, watching movies with her family, or curled up with a book.

She resides in Delaware with her husband and three children.

Visit her at www.jljackola.com and be sure to sign up for J L's newsletter to keep up with all the latest news.

www.ingramcontent.com/pod-product-compliance
Lightning Source LLC
Chambersburg PA
CBHW031039310726
48969CB00007B/2047